MY BAD BOY ALPHA

MONSTERS OF DURNBONE

EMILIA ROSE

CHAPTER
ONE

ZURI

"HE'S HERE," my coworkers whispered among each other, peering behind the doorframe and into Caelfall's most popular restaurant at the most feared man in town.

Alpha Stone had supposedly come all the way from Durnbone to find his fated mate.

A prophecy spoken long, long ago had promised that once he mated her, they'd be the most powerful couple in all of existence. In this space and this time, they would burn the forests to the ground, dine on the richest wine and the finest steaks, and have men and women falling to their knees in fear.

La-de-da-de-da.

Something like that.

All I knew was that I wanted to stay far away from him and his packmates. Elders had told me and my sister one too many horror stories about how his father and grandfather had ruled this land years ago.

But after the recent war of the wolves, his family had lost it all. Now, he planned to get it back. And I sorta felt sorry for the woman who'd be mated to him. I wouldn't be able to handle the hatred in his soulless eyes, the torture I'd have to witness.

Plus, I heard he was sick in the head … during sex.

"Zuri!" Sophia, my manager, called. "You're assigned to his table. Get out there."

Me?! Why has she chosen me of all people? That is usually Eshe's table!

"Can you, um"—I gulped and readjusted the button on my shirt—"get Eshe to do it?"

"Come on, Zuri," Sophia said, nudging me. "It's just a table, and besides … I bet he'll leave a nice tip for you. I heard he's rolling in money back in Durnbone, has the largest pack house anyone has ever seen."

I opened and shut my mouth, nerves bubbling up inside me. "Please, I don't want to."

"Get out of my way," Eshe said from behind me, shoving me to the side. "I'll do it." She retied her black apron around her petite figure, and then she pushed out her perky tits and plastered the fakest smile on her face. "It's not like he'd actually want to see you. He's here to find a mate, not a—"

"Eshe!" Sophia growled as if she knew what was about to leave my sister's mouth.

Eshe walked out the door and hurried toward Alpha Stone's table.

"Don't listen to her," Sophia said, offering me a smile. "She's a bitch." She poked me in the shoulder. "But you need to have some more confidence in yourself. I had you at his table so you could maybe …"

"Maybe what?" I asked. "Have someone in this town look at me the same way they look at Eshe and not …" My throat closed, and I couldn't even finish the sentence out loud.

Everyone here looked at me with disgust. Like I was some vile fiend.

Even though I could keep up with my pack during runs, even though I was strong on the training field, people—who were supposed to have my back—couldn't get over the way that I looked. It didn't matter what they said. I could see it in their eyes.

In their passive glances.

"You know …" She smiled. "Maybe."

If she knew how rude Eshe was, part of me wondered why she didn't just fire Eshe, but that was the stupid, selfish side of me. A side that I would never allow to come out because I feared losing my job. Eshe stayed in her position because she made the restaurant a lot of money and even more in tips.

Not because she was nice to the customers, but because my sister was beautiful.

In every single way that I'd never be.

A bell rang behind me, signaling that an order was ready. Deciding that I couldn't hide from the pack of rebels for much longer, I grabbed a tray of drinks for another table and hurried out into the rowdy main hall.

The thick scent of lavender drifted through my nose. And while I wanted to keep myself small and hidden as much as I could—that had always proven to be hard for me because I was a bigger, taller girl who was clumsy as shit—I couldn't stop myself from following the scent with my eyes and locking gazes with Stone from across the room.

My wolf, who I had buried deep inside to protect, suddenly awoke. *"Mate."*

Black tattoos covered every inch of his arms and neck, curling around his strong jaw and crawling into the fade of his modern mullet. Heat exploded in my core. His eyes were as dark as the midnight sky during a new moon, so vicious that they seized me by the damn throat.

My wolf raged against my insides, begging me to drop the tray and walk over to him, talk to him, *claim* him so she could be happy again. But I … I couldn't. My gaze shifted to Eshe, who placed her hand on his shoulder.

Jealousy and pain cut through my heart. I couldn't talk to him because I … because I would never be as beautiful as Eshe, would never have hair as silky, a straight smile, an uncrooked nose.

Caught in a panic, I tripped over a chair leg, and the tray slipped from my hand. Drinks flew in the air and splattered all over Alpha Connor, a visiting alpha, and the other high-ranking warrior wolves of the Stonehelm Pack.

"Oh my Goddess!" I shrieked, grabbing a napkin from the table and wiping it against his stained white shirt.

Goddess, why was I so freaking clumsy?! Last time I had bumped into Connor, he had nearly killed me for nicking his leather shoe. Now this?!

"I'm so sorry!"

I bowed my head and continued to attempt to clean his clothes with a pathetic napkin, hoping that he showed mercy on me. But … how could he? He was in the middle of dinner while one of the strongest alphas was in town.

Connor would want to show off, to assert his dominance.

Like I expected, Alpha Connor seized me by the throat, yanked me away from him, and pushed me back. "Get off me, you filthy omega." He grabbed his full glass of New Moon Shine, dumped it all over my head, and shoved me to the ground. "Lick it up like the ugly—"

Before Alpha Connor could finish his sentence, Alpha Stone was suddenly at my side, his dark eyes suddenly golden pools. He snatched Connor by the neck, slammed him up against the wall, and ripped out his throat in one fluid motion, as if he had done it a thousand times before. I stared in horror at the ripped spinal cord hanging from Stone's blood-covered fist.

"If anyone else wants to make a comment, you can suffer the same fate too," he growled through his vicious canines at the corpse. Then, he lifted his gaze to the other men around the table. "Nobody talks to my mate that way."

CHAPTER
TWO

STONE

"M-M-MATE?" she squeaked. With coily brown hair that she had pinned back with some gold hair clips, dark brown eyes, and the sexiest body that I had ever laid my eyes upon, she cowered back in fear and stared up at me through trembling eyes. "I'm your mate?"

"You speak as if you don't want the title," I growled.

She shook her head. "I-I can't be your m-mate."

Her words cut like an alpha's claws in my side. I had been searching my entire life for her, for the woman who would be by my side for the rest of my life. I had destroyed entire packs, burned their lands to the ground in a damn attempt to find her.

"Why not?" I snarled between my canines.

I didn't care what answer she had for me. She'd be—

"Because ... I'm not good enough for you."

For a moment, my words completely escaped me. I had expected some sob story about how she would never mate someone like me, a monster, as many people had called me over the years. That she was somehow better than some brute.

But she ... didn't think she was good enough? For me?

"Don't say that," I roared.

"It's true," she said.

And some fucking women to my right had the audacity to nod with her. *Fucking nod.*

I contained myself before I ripped their heads off too.

My mate might've had the worst self-esteem in this town, but once I was finished with her, those words would never come out of her mouth again. She wouldn't walk around, stumbling over her words and her own two feet.

She'd be the confident mate promised to me.

The woman I'd burn down the entire world for.

Mine.

When I snatched her chin in my rough hand, she flinched. I ignored it and forced her to stare up into my eyes. I wanted her to know that she would be mine, no matter what it took, no matter who I had to fight, no matter who I had to kill.

"You're mine," I growled.

"*She's* your mate?!" a woman shrieked from behind me.

I had never laid my hands on a woman, but my fingers twitched at the mere sound of her voice, the disgusted tone of it. I tugged my mate behind me, my canines lengthening as I turned around to face my waitress from earlier.

"Mine," I growled through my canines at her face, riddled with horror and disgust.

She bared her canines at the woman behind me, eyes blazing black, the way wolves' eyes were right before a battle during war.

"Do you have a problem with that?"

"I-I didn't know, Eshe," my mate cried behind me. "I'm sorry. I'm so sorry."

"Sorry for what?" I growled back at her.

"For being y-your mate," she whispered. She didn't say it out of disgust, but out of pure fear.

Her gaze was locked on to Eshe's, her eyes trembling. My mate wrapped her arms around her curvy body, which I couldn't wait to feast on tonight, lips quivering.

"You'd better be," Eshe snarled, hurling her foot forward.

I caught it before she touched my mate and tossed her back with ease. She smacked hard against a table, the wood breaking into two pieces and all the glasses shattering all over her, as she deserved.

"Don't fucking touch her," I growled.

Eshe stood and glared at me. "Do you see her?"

"Yes. And?"

"Do you think someone like her could ever be luna to *your* pack?!"

Teeth gritting together, I stepped forward. "Would you like to clarify?"

"Look at her!" Eshe said.

Suddenly, the room erupted into whispers of disgust that she was mine. A woman who they all claimed was ugly—with a crooked nose, oily skin, who was too tall, too clumsy, too curvy—was somehow not enough for me.

Though … these fuckers knew nothing about me.

Moments before I lunged forward to end them all, a hollow sob escaped my mate's mouth. She slapped a hand over her mouth to muffle her cries, but tears wavered in her eyes. Whatever they were saying through their mind link was hurting her.

Intentionally.

A roar of fury escaped through my canines. Blind rage.

I wanted to murder every last one of them, but I needed to get her out of here before I did. I wanted her to watch me do it, to show her that I was devoted to her, but whatever they said to her through the mind link was hurting her more.

"Find me everything you can about this pack, about my mate, and about this restaurant," I growled through my mind link to my beta, James.

Then, I grabbed my mate's hand. "You're coming with me."

"With you?" she repeated, sniffling. "B-but I have to—"

"You're not going to give me any excuses," I said, snatching her jaw and brushing my thumb across her lower lip. "You're mine whether you like it or not, darling. And I'm going to fucking devour every inch of your body tonight."

She held her hands over her stomach. "N-no."

After stepping toward her, I narrowed my dark gaze. "No?"

"I-I'm sorry. I didn't mean that. What I mean—"

Before she could get another word out, I picked her up and tossed her over my shoulder with ease, my hand coming down on her ass. "I'll be back to take care of this … fucking train wreck of a town, but you're mine tonight."

ZURI

A CURVY WOMAN like me was never supposed to be mated to such a cut and chiseled alpha. All the girls from high school had made sure I knew I'd end up alone or with a lone wolf, never accepting the fact that I was different from them and the other skinny girls in our pack.

And part of me stupidly believed those rumors, even after we had graduated and gotten on with our lives. Their words haunted me every single time I looked in the mirror, no matter how much I tried to love all my imperfections, all those stretch marks, and all that extra weight on my stomach.

But as fate would have it, I was mated to the sexiest, most ruthless alpha in this part of the forest. Nobody dared to mention the name of the cruel, tattooed, pierced man or else there would be consequences. Terrible consequences.

Yet here I was, alone in his bedroom, after he had brought me to his pack in Durnbone with one of his tattooed hands around my throat and the other between my legs, shoving his fingers into my wet pussy.

"Tell me what they said to you," he said, biting down on my

lower lip and thrusting his pierced tongue into my mouth for me to suck. "Tell me fucking everything that you've been told about your body. Tell me how you don't fucking love it, so I know how long I need to keep you here, touching, loving, worshipping every fucking inch of you until you do."

I couldn't remember how I had ended up in his bedroom with him touching me like this, but as soon as we had made it to the pack house, he was all over me, and I couldn't stop it. I didn't want to stop it either.

My heart raced, and I … I parted my lips, not knowing how to respond. All I had wanted earlier was to do my work as a waitress. I hadn't thought they'd bully me *in front* of Stone. I hadn't thought he'd come barreling to my rescue, looking for trouble and finding me—his mate—instead. And I sure as hell hadn't thought that I'd make it back to his pack house, half-naked and sopping wet at the thought of him being inside of me.

"Please," I whispered, grasping his wrist for him to stop because I was about to come undone already but secretly loving every moment of this pleasure. "It's okay. I don't mind," I said, knowing that if I told him all my truths, he'd lose it.

He was the cruelest alpha here; he had done murderous things to so many different people. Bullies were bullies, but I didn't want them to die. Maybe I did just a little, but not in the ways that he would kill them. He'd torture them for hours upon hours, and I didn't want anyone to feel that way. Maybe I was too nice.

"You know who I am, don't you?" he asked, fingers still furiously pumping into me. He sucked my bottom lip into his mouth and let it go with a pop.

"Yes," I breathed, my legs starting to shake in pleasure.

"Say my name."

"I can't," I whispered.

I had never spoken it a day in my life. Saying his name was forbidden in my pack. People were punished for it … because everyone thought that speaking the devil alpha's name would summon him.

And it had come true.

Yesterday, my alpha had spoken his name, and today, he had shown up at the restaurant!

"Say it," he said.

"Alpha ..."

"Alpha?"

"Stone," I said, my voice just above a whisper.

"And you know I don't fucking allow that kind of shit to happen to anyone I care about, don't you?"

His fingers curled around my G-spot, and I grasped his muscular shoulder through his tight gray sweater, my legs shaking uncontrollably. "I know ... oh Goddess, please don't stop."

He massaged my G-spot with his two fingers as his thumb worked its magic over my clit.

"I'm going to take care of them," he said, flicking his finger right over my clit and making me come for him.

Wave after wave of pleasure rushed through my body, and I leaned back on the bed, trying to ride out my orgasm.

He stood up, stuck his fingers in his mouth, and groaned. "Get on the bed," he said, voice husky.

I raised my brows and scrambled further up onto the mattress, my heart nearly pounding out of my chest. Moon Goddess ... what had I gotten myself into? I should've refused to come with him to his pack.

He walked to the headboard and picked up a piece of black rope tied to the bottom of it.

My eyes widened, and I went to pull myself away. "I'm not going to leave while you're gone. I promise."

He chuckled. "Oh, this isn't to keep you here," he said, tying it around my wrist. "If you left, I'd follow that pretty little scent of yours and drag you back to me. I've been waiting ages for you. You're not getting away."

"Then ... why are you tying me up?" I whispered.

After tying my wrists and ankles each to a bedpost and blindfolding me, he crawled on top of me, his breath on my neck, right where I ached for his mark. "I'll be back," he said, not answering me, but instead slipping something small and smooth into my tight panties.

"Where are you going?" I asked, tugging on the restraints and staring into the dark blindfold.

I felt so exposed. Being here, almost naked, felt like this was all some sick joke. How could my mate be the most feared alpha around, and how the hell could he want me?

He walked away. "To take care of those assholes who were fucking with you."

And before the door closed, that small and smooth thing between my legs began vibrating right against my clit, making me jump in surprise. I listened to the door close and tried hard not to make a sound, but the vibrations were more intense than any toy I'd used on myself before.

The pressure rose in my core, and I squeezed my eyes shut, begging myself to breathe evenly. Yet the pleasure was already surging through every single piece of my body, making me feel things that I shouldn't feel the first day I'd met my mate.

Pleasure rushed through me, hitting me hard and making me come. I pulled on the restraints, unable to deal with the heat between my legs, and tried to shift around to displace it. But the vibrations kept coming.

I must've been lying in that bed for at least an hour, trying to hold off the orgasms with thoughts about how the hell I had gotten here. But those racing thoughts didn't get rid of the coming orgasms.

CHAPTER
FOUR

STONE

"ESHE IS ZURI'S SISTER," James said to me, jogging to keep
up with my pace.

By nightfall, we, along with a couple of other warriors from
my pack, had run in our wolf forms all the way back to this shitty
town from Durnbone. I slowed my pace when I spotted the
restaurant, still bustling, even late into the night.

I had promised to return.

With revenge.

Soft yellow light glowed through the glass windows. I lengthened my nails into sharp claws once more, still feeling the dirt
from our run underneath them. I would slaughter every last one
of them for what they had done to Zuri.

For what her own sister had done.

Calling her names. Shouting at her in disgust. Attempting to
kick her.

And these fuckers were just going to let it happen. The alpha
and this pack had no respect for her because if they had, nobody
would have been treating her that way. Packs were supposed to
be fucking family.

Not bullies.

"I don't give a fuck who Eshe is to Zuri," I growled. "Zuri is your new luna and my mate."

James nodded and looked back to the others. "You know what to do."

Deciding that I wouldn't wait any longer, I kicked the door open and stepped into the room, commanding silence. The visitors paused, small murmurs erupting from the back. And then the pack members began running toward the doors before I could say a single word.

They pushed and pulled on the doors and attempted to escape through the windows, but my warriors had barricaded them into the wooden building. We allowed for no escape. A pack like this must be purged.

A flame of fire licked the outskirts of the building, crawling underneath the door and igniting the wooden floorboards. Men and women screamed for mercy, the same ones who had been murmuring about Zuri earlier.

Eshe ran my way. "Alpha Stone, you have to—"

I snapped my hand around her jaw and smirked at the pathetic woman. "Have to?"

"Get us out of here!"

"We're going to burn here together."

"You're going to burn in here with us?" she cried. "You've gone mad!"

"Only those who've sinned burn," I snarled, the heat crawling up my limbs.

"You murdered an alpha this morning, and you're talking about sin?!"

"A deal with the devil goes a long way." I smirked. "Burn in Tartarus, bitch."

I tossed her into the fire. Flames engulfed the room, burning bodies, the roar of the fire louder than the screams of dying wolves. I hoped that nobody in this pack fucking survived. They all deserved to be shit on for the rest of eternity.

Once the building burned to a crisp, I stood in the ashes with the blood of Eshe all over my naked body. A woman sprinted up the walkway to the old, dried-up wooden building that would never be a place where packs could bully my mate again.

"My … my restaurant!" the woman cried, falling to her knees when she reached the pile of ashes that she had once called *work*. Tears streamed from her cheeks. "What have you done?! I just went out for some asparagus."

My lips curled into a smirk. "What Zuri should've done years ago."

"Y-you're …" She opened and closed her mouth, as if choosing her next words carefully.

As if what she said would sway my mind.

"I'm what?" I asked, stepping closer to her. "Insane? Mad? Try again."

"That's not what I was going to … to say," she said. "Please."

"Please what?"

"Please don't hurt me."

Another step toward her. "And why would I do that?"

"I-I'm one of her friends," she said, backing up with her hands in the air. "I promise. I—"

I snatched her by the throat, completely engulfed by blind rage, and lifted her into the air. "Sophia Lamb, the owner of this restaurant and the manager of the employees. If you were her friend, you would've terminated Zuri's sister immediately."

How fake could someone be?

All these people, feeding my mate bullshit and forcing her to believe things about herself that weren't even close to being true. Once I was done cleaning up this mess, her ex-pack was next because a toxic work environment should *never* be tolerated by an alpha.

I didn't give a fuck what pack she belonged to. I would kill her alpha myself.

"I know," she said, bowing. "She will be fired."

"She was here, serving tables, when I returned!" I growled

through my canines. "She's already been fired because she's dead. Because of me. And any attempt to rebuild your little restaurant will cease to exist because of me too."

"No!" she screamed at the top of her lungs. "Don't do it! Please! I have a—"

Locking one hand to the top of her head and the other to her jaw, I ripped her head from her body and snarled as the headless corpse fell to the ground with a thud. I would do anything for my mate.

Anything.

ZURI

WHEN THE DOOR OPENED AGAIN, there was complete silence. Then, I heard that low, sinister chuckle that both sent shivers down my spine and made me clench and ache in all the right places.

"Look at you," he said, walking into the room. He hooked a finger into my underwear, pulled gently, and let it slap against my hip. "How many times have you come without my permission?" he asked, pulling the vibrator out of my panties and tossing it.

All I could smell was the stench of blood all over him. What had he done?

Suddenly, he slapped a hand down on my clit, and I gasped, pressure building up inside me.

"How many times?" he asked. When I didn't answer him, he slapped my pussy again, pulled apart my folds, and tasted me himself, his tongue ring flicking against my sensitive and swollen clit. "How many fucking times?"

"Three," I whispered, pulling on the restraints. My mind was telling me that I really shouldn't be here because he was batshit crazy … but my wolf and I wanted to be devoured by our mate. "What'd you do to them?" I asked before I could stop myself.

His pierced tongue flicked out against my clit again, hitting me exactly where I needed it, and I moaned out loud, pleasure rushing to my core. He pushed a finger into me and pumped it in and out of me slowly.

"All you need to know is that I took care of them for you, baby." He pulled the blindfold off me and finally let me see him.

Lying between my legs, he stared up at me with those dark brown–almost black–eyes that almost looked black from this angle. One hand was sprawled over my stomach, gripping and tugging on it gently.

"No more questions," he said, resting my thighs on his muscular, tattooed shoulders. Every muscle in his abdomen was flexed hard as he pumped his fingers into me again. "Lie back and be a good girl for me."

He flicked his tongue over and over against my clit, his tongue ring rubbing against it and making me clench even harder. I squirmed under him, my hips moving from side to side as he continued to eat my pussy until I was about to come again.

But just as I was about to, he stopped, slapped my clit, and stared down at me with those cold yet devouring eyes. After crawling off the bed, he undid the rope around my ankles and started to unbuckle his belt, pulling it off and tossing it onto the bed next to me. I watched him tug the button off and push down his pants, leaving him just in his tight gray briefs.

He was hard, his huge cock pressing against the thin material. I swallowed, feeling the heat warm my core, and bit my lip. Goddess, he was going to be inside of me tonight. Alpha Stone would be filling me with his thick cock, pounding into me, loving me.

Once he pushed down his briefs, he wrapped his hand around his cock and walked over to me, climbing onto the bed and rubbing the head of his pierced cock on my lips. "Get the head wet for me, baby."

He thrust a couple of inches of himself into my mouth, and I wrapped my lips around his head, my tongue flicking out against his cock ring. He groaned against me, his hand laced into my hair.

"Fuuuck," he said, reaching between my legs and fingering my pussy again as I sucked him off.

All I could hear were the wet sounds coming from me that were meant for him.

"I'm going to fuck you so fucking good, baby," he said, pushing his cock a bit deeper down my throat. "Make sure that you know I love every single inch of you."

When my pussy tightened around his fingers, he smirked.

"Please," I tried to say, but he only pushed himself deeper until he was almost hitting the back of my throat and making me gag. I stared up into his dark eyes, taking in those tattoos that covered his body and that tongue ring that I could see just past his parted lips.

He pulled himself out of my throat, stuck his wet fingers into my mouth, and said, "Suck my fingers like a good fucking girl."

Willingly, I sucked off my juices. He grasped his cock, stroking it roughly, and crawled between my legs, letting the head of him brush against my entrance. He left sloppy, wet kisses from my breasts to my neck, and when he reached my throat, he paused and let his canines brush against my soft spot.

"Mine. You're fucking mine. Nobody else touches you. Nobody else looks at you. Nobody fucking bullies you again." He grasped my chin roughly in his hand and forced me to look into those dark eyes. "Tell me you understand, baby."

My heart pounded as I stared at those long, vicious canines, my wolf just waiting for them to be inside of me. He pressed the head of his dick against my entrance.

When I didn't answer, he growled, "Tell me."

"I understand," I whispered.

And then he thrust his long, hard cock right inside me. Inch by inch, he pushed himself into me until he was balls deep.

"Stuffed full," he groaned into my ear. "Your pussy feels so fucking good."

I clenched around him and moaned out loud, arching my back, the pressure rising in my core so damn quickly. I had never been with a man like him, never been with someone who wanted me to know just how much more I deserved and who would defend me without even knowing me.

"I'm going to come," I whispered, squeezing my eyes closed.

He sucked one of my nipples into his mouth, the metal from his tongue ring flicking out against the hard bud, and pounded harder into me. My legs started to shake, but I kept my feet planted on the mattress.

He tugged on my nipple, his teeth biting hard into it, and let it go. I squirmed in his hold, unable to stay still as wave after wave of pleasure rolled through me. After a few moments, he stilled inside of me and grunted against my ear. I relaxed against his body and closed my eyes, the pleasure making my legs tingle in delight.

"Mine," he growled against my lips. "You're mine now."

CHAPTER
SIX

STONE

THE NEXT MORNING, Zuri lay on my bed, cuddled up with the pillows and sheets. I walked into the room with a tray of the best food that the pack cooks could make. They had brought some over earlier after news that I had found my mate spread like wildfire through the pack.

She sat up and leaned against the headboard, pulling the sheets up to hide her naked body from me. I hid my canines behind my lips and bit back a growl. Every time she did that, it pissed me off even more.

"Here," I said, handing her a glass of tea and a pastry. "Drink this. It will help you recover."

After eyeing it for a moment, she grabbed the glass and took a huge gulp. "What is it?"

"It's tea I bought specifically for you from a trinket shop in downtown Durnbone."

"A trinket shop?" she asked, brow furrowed. "They have tea at a trinket shop?"

"It's a special kind of tea … and shop for that matter," I hummed, tilting the glass up so she would drink more of it.

She took another long sip and licked her lips, handing me the cup. I placed it on the tray.

"It's for pregnancy."

She choked on the tea, eyes wide. "Y-you mean, birth control, right?"

"No," I said. "It's to better the odds of you getting pregnant with our child."

"What?!"

"Baby, I know you heard me loud and clear," I said, setting the glass on the tray and then heading toward the closet to find clothes for today. I planned on ripping her ex-alpha to shreds at some point, but wanted to spend time with her.

War would come later.

"Finish eating," I commanded. "Then, get dressed. We have plans."

"Stone!" she exclaimed. "Are you serious?!"

"Dead serious, baby."

After her initial surprise, she finally set the tray on the bed next to her legs and grasped the blankets tighter to her chest. "But I don't have anything to wear, and I doubt that they'll have any clothes for me in Durnbone at this hour."

"You've never been to Durnbone, have you?" I asked.

"No."

"People here don't give a shit about how you look, especially after the new demon king rose to power a few months ago," I said. "There are people of all shapes, sizes, colors, and species here. They'll have clothes for you."

"But it's early morning."

I tore off my shirt and tossed it to her. "Then, you'll wear mine until we can go shopping."

She dropped her gaze to my torso, pupils dilating, then whimpered softly. "It won't fit."

A low growl escaped my mouth. "Come here."

While she scurried out of the bed, she didn't follow my orders, but instead waltzed to the mirror with the sheets still wrapped around her body and my shirt in her hand. She stared at herself for a few moments, then tried to maneuver herself in a way where she could pull on the shirt, but not drop the blanket.

The blanket fell anyway, and I had to control myself so I wouldn't dump another load of cum deep in her pussy. Goddess, she was the sexiest fucking thing that I had ever laid my eyes on. No wonder those assholes of pack members had made fun of her —they were all jealous.

"Dress," I ordered, lips curling into a smirk. "Unless you want to walk around naked."

She squealed and wiggled into the shirt before I could get a long look. "Goddess, no."

"I wouldn't mind it." I leaned against the wall and crossed my tattooed arms, watching her fiddle with my shirt. "I'd walk you around my pack and show you off to everyone so they'd fume with jealousy because you're mine."

Cheeks flushing, she gawked at me in horror. "Why would you do that? You're an alpha."

"And?"

"Alphas are the most possessive and jealous animals by nature," she said. "Alpha Nurx would kill anyone who even looked at his mate in the wrong way, especially when she got close to heat. Why would you want anyone to look at me? Naked?!"

"Because you're sexy as fuck," I growled. "And if any *pup* wants to challenge me for you because of it, then I will rip out his throat and feed it to his family." I stepped closer to her, wrapped my hand around her throat, and pinned her to the wall. "You're mine, Zuri. All mine."

Her lips trembled, yet an unreadable expression crossed her face. "Y-yours?"

"Until you take your last breath."

"And what will happen until then? What will you do with me?"

I lifted her chin with my fingers. "Anything *you* want me to do."

She paused for a moment and pressed her thighs together, the heat radiating from her tight little cunt. I growled and dropped my gaze to her legs, my dick throbbing inside my pants. I needed to breed her, to get her pregnant so she wouldn't even *think* about leaving me, about not wanting to be my mate.

"What did you really do to them?" she finally asked. "My pack?"

Honestly, with the way she had reacted earlier and was acting now, I wasn't sure she really wanted to know. But she was my mate now. She would see the monster I was and accept it whether she wanted to or not.

"They are not your pack anymore," I declared. "You're protected by *my* pack."

"B-but what d-did you do to them?" she repeated, eyes widening. "D-did you kill them?"

"You really want to know?" I asked.

"Yes."

My lips curled more into a smile. "Come then. I brought a gift from your ex-pack home with me last night. I'll show you what happened."

CHAPTER
SEVEN

ZURI

I SHOOK IN HORROR. "NO."

"No?" Stone repeated. "You don't even know what it is."

"I know that whatever this present is, it's nothing good," I murmured, heart racing. I had heard horror stories of him, had seen how he devoured me last night until I passed out from too much pleasure. "I don't want it."

Stone stared blankly at me for a couple of moments, and then his sharp jaw twitched. "Zuri."

"Stone."

Clenching his jaw, he growled underneath his breath and drew his tongue across his large canines. "I don't care if you want it or not. You're going to take it one way or another. Come with me."

"N-no."

While I didn't know *exactly* what it was because I had been told to fear Stone all my life, he made me feel safe to speak my mind more than I felt around my ex-pack. Although I did and even though he was an alpha—the most *feared* alpha around these parts—I felt like I could say anything, no matter how bratty and pissed I was.

He pursed his lips, and then his eyes glazed over, as if he was listening to someone through his mind link. When he finally came back, he blew out a low breath and left the room without saying another word.

And while I had told him I didn't want to see his present, I didn't want to stay here alone. I didn't know who would walk in, didn't have any food left besides the pregnancy tea that he had forced me to drink this morning.

"Wait!" I said, finding some shorts in his dresser and tugging them up my legs.

Once I was dressed—sorta—I hurried out of the room and wandered down the large hallway that seemed to stretch on forever. I peered into the empty guest rooms, a lounge room with a huge gray beanbag, some video game controllers, and a glass-door fridge full of Fudgsicles.

I eyed them for a moment, then thought against it and continued down the hallway, following his lingering scent. My wolf was relaxing for the first time in years, purring at the thought of him being inside her again. Making me wet and uncomfortable in these clothes.

Voices drifted from the first floor. I tiptoed down the stairs, amazed that *anyone* like Stone lived in such a … normal house. I had expected skulls posted on every door, walls splattered in blood, bones as decorations.

"What's next?" a man said in the next room.

"You know what's next," Stone growled. "The beginning of an empire."

"Where do you want to start?" the man said. "With Alpha Calder?"

"We don't touch him. Not yet. His mate is too strong."

Stone wasn't scared of her, but definitely cautious. And me? Well, I might've been sorta, kinda jealous of her, and I didn't even know the woman. Nobody had ever told me how strong I was, not even any of my old packmates.

"Thanks for bringing this," Stone said.

And I almost passed out because I hadn't known that this man had manners. Between bringing me tea that would get me pregnant this morning to doing Goddess only knew what to my packmates last night … I hadn't thought I'd hear those words ever leave his mouth.

I wanted to peek around the corner of the doorframe to see what exactly he had thanked this random man for. Maybe it was someone's head? The spinal cords of his enemies, wrapped up like a bouquet? I didn't put it past him.

"Zuri," Stone taunted, "you don't have to hide."

I peered around the doorframe and spotted the same man I had seen with him last night at the restaurant.

Blond hair, puppy-dog brown eyes, and muscular, he smiled at me and bowed his head. "Luna, it's so nice to meet you."

"Zuri," Stone announced, "this is my beta, James. James, Zuri."

Scurrying out from behind the wall, I awkwardly stood next to Stone in nothing but his T-shirt and a pair of shorts. All I wanted to do was go hide in his room and never come out. Goddess, it had been hard enough, getting *some* respect from my old packmates, and now, I had to do it all over again.

Not something I really wanted to do.

"I hope you had a good sleep last night," he said with a small smile. "My mate is so excited to meet you. She was talking about it all night, wouldn't let me get to bed." He chuckled. "Anyway, she brought over some food for you this morning."

My eyes widened slightly. Why was he being so nice?

When he waited for my response, I cleared my throat and smiled back. "It was lovely."

Stone curled his arm around my waist and pulled me closer until my body was pressed gently against his rippling muscles. I sucked in a sharp breath, loathing the fact that we were so close in front of another person.

But James didn't say anything about it.

After another grin, he stuffed his hands into his pockets and nodded to a box on the table. "If you need any more of that, Stone, let me know. We didn't know how much you needed, so I had the others bring home a couple of boxes."

"This is enough," Stone said. "Just enough to fill a bath for my mate."

Stiffening, I peered up at the smirk painted across Stone's face and then toward the box. My stomach twisted and turned, my insides uneasy about whatever the hell was in this container. For all I knew, it was more of that damn pregnancy juice that he'd make me sit in for hours so I could get pregnant with his pups.

No, thank you.

I didn't know what kind of facade they were all putting on, but I didn't trust it at all.

Stone's pack wasn't nice, and he was even less so. He was a villain who had destroyed packs just to find me, take me, and then break me into small pieces. So I would bend my knee and obey him.

After nodding at me, James exited the house and shut the front door behind himself. Stone grabbed the box in one hand and my hand in the other, leading me back into the maze of hallways and into a large bathroom that could easily fit five she-wolves along with him.

"Is this where you invite your pack?" I hummed.

"You think very poorly of me," he said, releasing my hand and beginning the water.

"Because you're not nice."

"You don't know me, Z." He opened the cardboard box and dumped the thin pieces of what looked like burned paper or petals into the warm bath water. Then, he held out his hand. "Take off your clothes and get in."

I stared down at the grayish water, then snapped my gaze back up to him. "What is it?"

"There was no blood for you to bathe in, so I brought you their ashes."

STONE

"WH-WHAT ARE YOU TALKING ABOUT?" Zuri stepped away from me, her fingers trembling and her lips quivering as she tried to enunciate more and more words. "Stone … whose ashes are these?"

"Your ex-packmates."

She doubled over onto her knees and puked up her breakfast all over the ground, clutching her stomach. When she lifted her head to look back up at me, she dropped her gaze to the bowl of ashes and then puked again.

"Y-you killed them?"

"No. I locked them in a building and burned it. If I had killed them, I would've brought you their heads, too, but … we're using the skulls for other matters." *That she probably doesn't want to know about.*

Once she finally came back up for air, she rolled over onto her ass and glared up at me through teary eyes. "Sophia was my manager!" Zuri shrieked. "And one of my friends. How could you do such a thing?!"

"Sophia was just as much your bully as they all were," I growled through my canines.

"She was nice to me," my mate argued.

But she had become so blind to it all, so used to the constant bullying from her packmates that she accepted any niceness. She couldn't see how fake Sophia was, couldn't understand that no matter how bad it had gotten, Sophia would've never fired Zuri's sister.

She hadn't cared about Zuri. Plain and simple.

"Being nice doesn't mean she was your friend," I said. "And it certainly doesn't mean that she deserved to live. She burned, just like the rest of them, and she died like all the men, women, demons, wolves, vampires that had been liars and cheats before her."

"But—"

"No friend could do that to you. And I won't allow anyone to treat you that way," I growled, refusing to give Zuri any less than what she deserved.

Fucking kindness—not being bullied and spit on, kicked and name-called—was what every creature deserved.

Not the shitty packmates that had called themselves Zuri's friends.

I crouched down in front of her. "Do you want to know why everyone fears me?"

"Because you're fucking psychotic!" she shrieked, scrambling back on her ass until she hit a wall. She wrapped her arms around her body and glared harder at me. "Trying to get me to bathe in my pack's ashes."

"Ex-pack," I corrected. "People who didn't give a fuck about you." I moved closer to her and grabbed her throat, tilting her head up so she stared up at me. "No, sweetheart. It's because I'm not afraid to do anything for the people—*for the woman*—I love."

"You don't love me," she said. "You don't even know me."

"I don't love you now, but I will."

She shuffled to her feet, then backed away from me and

stretched out her arm toward me, holding up her hand. "N-no, you … we … you can't love me. I'm not a monster like you. I can't be mated to someone who kills people for fun."

"I don't kill people for fun," I said. "I kill them because they don't deserve to live."

"I've heard of your plans to rule an empire of wolves," she whispered, staring at me through large, tear-filled eyes. She wrapped her arms around herself and shook her head. "Is it true? Do you plan on eliminating everyone who stands in your path, like you did with my … my family?"

I growled at the word because that had been no family, but responded with, "Yes."

While I had been blind with rage late last night, a different emotion that I had never felt before built higher and higher inside me. I dipped my head into the crook of her neck, breathing in the intoxicating scent of my mate.

"And I'm going to give you the fucking world," I growled. "You're mine."

She sucked in a sharp breath. "Stone—"

"Say it."

"No."

I drew my canines across her neck and gently pricked them into her skin, not enough to mark her yet, but enough for her to know that she was mine. That there was no escaping this. No escaping me.

"Say it," I growled.

"N—"

"Don't make me order you again, mate. Or I'll drag you back up to that bedroom and show you who you belong to," I snarled. "I'll make you *beg* for me on your knees with my cock down your pretty little throat and your eyes filled with tears. So, fucking say it." I tightened my hand around her throat and stared down into those pretty brown eyes. "You know I will—"

"I'm yours," she finally breathed.

"Forever," I growled.

CHAPTER
NINE

ZURI

STONE DRAGGED his teeth across my neck, his warm breath giving me chills. I wasn't supposed to like any part of this, but my wolf wanted him to touch me everywhere, like he had last night, except this time with his canines.

Heat coursed through my body, and I pressed my thighs together, biting back a moan.

Stop it, Zuri. He's a villain. A monster. My mate.

My entire body froze, and I stared down at the bath of ashes. My mate was a pure monster who wanted nothing more than to have me bathe in the ashes of the wolves I had once thought of as family, friends, packmates.

Even if they hadn't liked me, even if they had constantly put me down, this was wrong.

So wrong.

"No," I growled, shoving him back. "Get away from me. You can't mark me. Not now."

I couldn't be mated to this beast. The Moon Goddess must've made a mistake, a wrong choice. No way would I ever be able to tame him. He had brought me ashes of my ex-pack, for fuck's sake! And *I* tried not to sob when someone said something mean to me.

In no world were we fated to be together!

Eyes glossy with lust, he stumbled back slightly and painted a smirk on his lips. "No?"

From the mere huskiness in his voice, I clenched and sucked in a breath. My body—my wolf—was doing everything in her power to get me to submit to him, to allow *him* to mark me. But, Goddess, did I fear him and everything he was capable of doing to *me*.

"Wipe that smirk off your face," I said, crossing my arms over my chest and attempting to act confident for once in my pathetic life. Except he could see right through me with those predator eyes. "You will not mark me because we can't be mates."

He chuckled darkly. "Is that so? I love a good challenge."

"I-it's not a challenge. You'll never be able to be the mate I want." *And need.*

A low growl escaped his lips, and he suddenly had me pressed against the nearest door. His large, muscular body against my chest, his dark eyes staring down at me. I stepped back in an attempt to disappear *through* the door.

"Try me, mate," he growled, a sudden roughness to his voice. "Come meet my pack."

My eyes widened even more. "Meet your pack?"

"Meet my pack," he repeated.

"No, I can't," I whispered, reaching behind myself to twist the doorknob.

When the door clicked open, I twirled around as quickly as my uncoordinated ass could and accidentally tumbled to the ground. After giving him a clear view of my vagina, I scrambled to my feet and hurried down the hallway.

The afternoon sun flooded through Stone's windows, creating patterns on the hardwood floor. I raced to the steps and then headed straight for his bedroom because it had a lock. I didn't trust myself with him anymore today.

We needed to be as far as—

Before I could slam the door in his face, he grabbed it with one hand and yanked it open with his brute force. I stared up at him, my heart pounding inside my chest, and stepped back. His eyes weren't as dark, but that same smirk was painted upon his face.

"Come with me," Stone demanded, holding out a large, tattooed hand toward me. "I'm going to introduce you to the pack. They deserve to meet and spend time with their luna as much as possible because in a couple of weeks, you'll be too worried about our pups growing in your belly to do much else."

My eyes widened. "What?! No!"

But he left me no room to disagree. What Alpha Stone said would happen—he'd proven that, even before I met him. This man could tell other packs what to do, and they'd do it because they were fucking terrified of him.

Me? Well, I wasn't that scared of him anymore. I had known him for a whopping one day, and he had done nothing but fuck me. No killing. No smacking. No choking—unless it was the good kind.

Still, no matter which bullies Stone killed for me, my insecurities weren't just … over in a matter of twenty-four hours. Those bullies had beaten into my head that I wasn't good enough, wasn't pretty enough, wasn't *enough* to be mated with anyone.

What would everyone think about Stone when they found out he was mated to someone like *me*? Would they all laugh in my face? Maybe that was what James, his beta, was doing right about now with his wife.

"Can't we wait for a couple more days … or months? You know …" I started.

I didn't know where I was going with it. I wasn't going to be ready to meet the pack within a couple of months. It would take years for me to be ready to face them without feeling bad about it. I was stuck between all those insecurities and self-love, and I hated it. I wished things would get easier every now and then.

Instead of taking my hand and dragging me out of the room,

like I expected him to do, he pulled me closer to him, snatched my chin between his fingers, and stared down with those dangerous eyes. "Why don't you want to meet them?"

"Because ..."

I didn't know what to say. I hated talking about my insecurities.

"I *know* why, but I want to hear you say it," he continued.

Not wanting to speak the words out loud because that would make them real, I shook my head and stared down at the ground, wiggling around my toes. "I just don't think I'm ready to meet them, Stone."

It was a lie, and he saw right through it.

And this man—Goddess, this man—was going to make me *pay* for lying to him.

CHAPTER
TEN

STONE

BEFORE I COULD START my next sentence—my next lie—he growled, "What do I have to do to get you to believe you're fucking sexy as hell?" And then he spun me around toward a mirror. "What do you see?" he asked me. When I didn't respond, he grabbed my chin and forced me to stare at myself in the mirror. "Answer me."

"I don't know," I said, voice barely audible.

"Tell me."

My gaze flickered behind me. "I—I see a man who deserves so much more than me."

Again, Stone let out another deadly growl. "Hands on the mirror. You're going to watch me love your body."

My pussy clenched, and I sucked in a sharp breath, placing my hands on the mirror and staring at him through the reflection. Still, that bullied part of me didn't accept that a man like Stone—the sexiest, most cutthroat alpha in all of the world—wanted *me*.

That was what it all really came down to. I didn't really fear him. I just thought that the Moon Goddess had made a mistake because he was wanted by everyone and I was wanted by nobody in the entire world.

He slid off my shorts and panties, and then he undid his bottoms and pushed them down to his knees, pulling out his huge cock and slapping it against my pussy. "I'm this hard for *you*, mate. Nobody else could ever make my cock fucking throb like this."

A wad of spit dripped from his mouth to his veiny cock. With his thumb, he rubbed the spit over his cock ring, making it glisten in the sunlight flooding into the room through the curtains. After stepping closer to me, he rubbed his head against my clit from behind.

I swallowed hard and sucked in a sharp breath, a wave of pleasure rushing through me.

Continuing to shove his dick between my pussy lips, he grabbed my hip in his other hand and grunted into my ear, the mere sound making me shudder in absolute pleasure already. "You've put this off for long enough," Stone growled. "After I fuck your desperate, aching cunt, you're meeting the pack. No shower. No cleaning my cum out of you. I want everyone in my pack to smell your pussy, filled with me."

My pussy clenched even harder, and Stone decided it was the perfect time to shove himself into my sopping cunt. He wrapped one hand around my throat and ripped my shirt down the middle, letting my breasts fall out of it.

After growling against my soft spot, he groped one in his hand. "Look at these tits. They're so fucking huge. I can't even fit one in my hand." He slapped it and made it bounce against the mirror. "You turn me the fuck on with everything you fucking do."

His hand slipped from around my throat and traveled down my body to my clit, rubbing against the sensitive bud. With his other hand, he hiked my leg up into the air, his biceps flexing. He stared at me through the reflection—not at my pussy or my tits or my body, but at me.

As he pounded his taut body into me from behind, I squeezed my eyes closed to focus on the pleasure building quickly between my legs.

He shoved himself as deep as he could go, stilled, and said, "Open up your eyes. I said that you were going to watch."

When I reopened my eyes, he started up once more, ramming his cock into my hole and staring intently at me through the reflection. His dark eyes turned into fiery golden pools, the way they had the other night at the restaurant.

It was the sinister side of him that everyone feared.

Everyone, except me.

"Oh my Goddess ..."

"Come on my cock, *mate.*"

My claws dug into the drywall. I threw my head back, my gaze still focused on those piercing eyes, and felt my legs tremble underneath me. He held me up with his brute strength as an orgasm ripped through my body harder and faster than it ever had before.

Wave after wave of pleasure shot through me, making my fingers and legs tingle.

"Fuck," he growled.

He stilled deep inside of me, grunting and cursing my name, telling me how good it felt.

When he pulled out of me, he tugged my panties up my thighs and rubbed his fingers against the silky material that had to quickly be getting wet, ruining them with all his cum that was dripping out of my hole.

I shuffled around, my core still throbbing, and pulled my shirt together. Stone stopped me, tied the bottom so my tits were nearly spilling out, then snatched my hands.

"Your tits are too nice to cover up. I want something to stare at today."

And with that, he dragged me out of the bedroom to meet his pack for the very first time.

CHAPTER
ELEVEN

ZURI

"PLEASE, STONE," I pleaded, dragging my feet like an immature brat.

It had been twenty-four hours since he had taken me, and I was still *attempting* to familiarize myself with his crazy ass. I didn't need an entire pack of people just like him right now. Honestly, I didn't know if I could handle that, especially after those ashes.

"You're meeting the pack," Stone said without argument.

"But—"

I snapped my mouth closed when he swung the front door open and tried not to sound like a bitch because I at least wanted the pack to like me. Stone marched us all the way down to a small river, where James stood with his mate, washing blood off her shoulder in the water.

"What happened?" Stone asked, canines lengthening. "Did Dirt attack?"

"Dirt?" I asked.

Damn, they really went all natural for the names around here, huh? Next, Stone would try to convince me to name our future pup Cloud or Sun. Nothing wrong with those names, but I didn't want my child to get bullied.

My cheeks flushed. Why the hell was I thinking about a pup right now?!

James glanced over his shoulder at us. "We call Stone's brother Dirt because he's ..."

"A piece of shit," Stone finished, clenching his jaw. "Now, what happened?"

"Just some roughhousing," James said, earning him a slap from his mate.

"James," she scolded, glaring at him for a moment. "Not in front of our new luna."

"What?" James argued. "It's not like—"

James's mate nudged him hard in the ribs, then smiled at me. "Sorry about him. You must be Luna Zuri." She stepped forward, bowed her head, then extended her arm for me to shake. "I'm Beta James's mate, Sapphire."

"It's nice to meet you," I said in a whisper.

Sapphire giggled. "You can call me Saph. Everyone around here does."

"Speaking of everyone," Stone interrupted because that man didn't have self-control and wanted me to meet every single member of his pack right this very instant. "Where's the pack? Training finished less than an hour ago. Most stay around until noon."

"I thought that our luna would need some ... time to adjust after your gift this morning," James said.

I placed my hands on my hips, arched a brow, and turned toward Stone. "See."

"See what?"

"He knew I needed time," I scolded in the happiest tone so Saph wouldn't judge me.

"Are you saying that my beta knows my mate better than I do?" he growled, his long canines glistening with saliva in the sunlight. He stepped toward me and grasped my chin, forcing me to crane my head up at him. "Hmm?"

My gaze dropped to his canines yet again, and I pressed my thighs together. *Fuck.*

Curse the Moon Goddess for these damn feelings. For making me ache for him.

"Answer m—"

"No," I said, pushing him off me and turning away.

I felt Stone's intense gaze on me for another moment, and then he looked toward the couple giggling in front of us.

"Gather everyone for dinner tonight then. Zuri will have had time to adjust. Right, Zuri?"

I crossed my arms, wanting to delay this for as long as possible. "No."

"Great." Then, Stone said to James, "We'll see everyone at six."

"What? No!" I exclaimed, twirling back around to see Stone inches from me now.

He took another step toward me, pushing me back with his large body, his dark eyes gazing so deep into my fucking soul that I swore he could steal it if he were the Devil.

"You're lucky today, mate. Earned yourself a couple more hours."

"B—"

Before I could protest—to *beg*—for more time, he scooped me up and threw me over his shoulder like I weighed nothing to him and marched toward the edge of his property. "We're heading to Durnbone for the day to pamper you."

———

After an hour massage that Stone had to sit in on—to make sure the masseur didn't *touch* me in any way that he didn't like—and some time at Durnbone's most luxurious salon, Stone brought me to shop for clothes.

I ambled around the stores with jealousy running through me. All the women stared at us—or to be more specific, at Stone. Yet he was more interested in the sluttiest clothes that he could find me to wear than some stares.

When we approached the cashier, he had picked out five outfits that were more like bikinis that he must've thought I was actually going to wear. Joke was on him because I had never swum in my entire life and there was no way in *hell* that I'd put those on.

"We'll take these," he said to the cashier.

She rang up the clothes and gazed behind us when the bell on the door clattered. I followed her gaze, spotting two women about my age walking into the shop, giggling with each other. Stone curled his arm around my waist.

"Do you know them?" I asked.

"Maxine and Sina," Stone said. "Maxine is the queen of demons, and Sina is …"

"What?" I asked.

He paused for a moment. "She's exceptionally strong and a human turned wolf, mated to four warriors east of Durnbone." He took my hand and squeezed it softly. "You don't need to worry about her."

"Did you date her?" I asked, jealousy pooling in my stomach.

"Fuck no," he growled.

"Then, why'd you say it like that?"

"Like what?"

"Like you're not telling me the whole truth."

"Because I don't want you getting messed up with Sina. She has powers that can be uncontrollable, and I can't let her hurt you. I'd start a world fucking war in Durnbone if anything happened to you."

My eyes widened slightly. "What kind of power—"

Before another word could leave my mouth, a blade whizzed through the air in the middle of the shop. Stone reached out his hand and caught the knife mid-throw, his palm wrapping around the metal and splitting open.

A shadowy figure stood behind the girls, leaning against the doorframe with one hand stuffed into his pocket and the other gripping a variety of knives.

Stone curled his lips into a smirk, tossing the knife into the air as blood dripped down his palm. "It's been a long time, *brother*."

STONE

"IS THIS DIRT?" Zuri whispered, tugging on my sleeve once I paid for her clothes.

A low chuckle left my mouth. "No, this isn't my piece-of-shit brother. This is Carve."

"Carve," she repeated, her face contorted into one of horror. She dropped her gaze to my palm that had split open from seizing the knife, watching as the wound healed almost instantly. "What kind of town is this? These names are ridiculous."

I chuckled again and leaned closer to her. "Don't tell him that."

She tensed and widened her eyes, inching closer to me.

After taking her hand, I led her to Maxine, Sina, and Carve. She was hesitant about meeting other people, but I still pulled her along because she needed to get over her fears one way or another.

"Stone," Carve said, nodding.

"Who's this?" Sina asked, smiling at Zuri.

"This is my mate, Zuri."

Zuri gulped and peered over at them. "H-hi."

"Hi!" Maxine waved from Sina's side. "Wanna grab coffee with us?"

"Um, I think we were—"

"Go," I said to her, ushering her along. "I need to talk to Carve alone."

Staring at me through huge *help me* eyes, Zuri sighed softly and followed the girls across the street to a small coffee shop named Chaos. I cleared my throat and walked with Carve out the doors.

"Haven't seen you in a few days," Carve said.

"Could say the same about you."

"What'd you ask me to meet you here for?"

"Advice," I said.

He let out a lifeless laugh. "Since when do you need advice?"

"Since you're the only person who has done what I want to do."

"Done what?"

"Rule the world."

"You want me to tell you how? Fuck no. Besides, you have a mate now."

"And?"

"And you should forget about your dreams, about revenge. It will lead you nowhere."

"Do you think any pack—especially my brother's—really deserves to live?" I asked, my hand tightening into a fist while I gazed past Carve and toward Zuri, who stood tensely next to Maxine and Sina across the street. "Zuri's ex-pack abused her—mentally, emotionally, and physically. Goddess only knows what my shit-faced brother will do once he finds out I have found my mate. I need to do—"

"You don't understand," he growled. "If you have done what I have done, killed who I have killed, lusted for power and women, validation, vengeance, then you would not attempt to slaughter your brother. That's a terrible path to walk down alone."

"I'm not alone. I have Zuri."

"And I had Olenna once."

I pressed my lips together and averted my gaze. "The rumors are lies. I don't lust for power or women. I lust after wrapping my hands around my brother's throat and feeling the way his blood pumps through his body while he takes his last breath."

"Do you think I was so terribly motivated when I began my journey?" he asked. "Because I had innocent motives that were corrupted over time by reality. Not dreams or people. Reality, Stone. If you don't take this shit seriously, you'll see for yourself."

I didn't take advice from anyone, but I respected Carve. He had lived a thousand lives, fought ten thousand battles, and lost his fated mate hundreds of times over and over again. Now, she lived in hatred of him.

Utter hatred.

"Olenna lives in Durnbone, you know," I said.

"Don't bring her up," he said through gritted teeth. "I know she does. I've seen her."

"Don't you want her back?"

"Of course I do. My eyes fucking burn every night while I watch her flirt with other men, lie with them in her bedroom," Carve snapped, hand tightening around his knives. "She is supposed to be with me, and I'm slowly losing control again around her. I fear that there will be no going back. No turning back time. This time ..."

"You'll have her for good," I finished.

He relaxed his grip on his knives and nodded in agreement, but we both knew that she wouldn't come to him willingly. He would have to wreak havoc, need to do shit so horrific that she couldn't ignore.

"We will be together until our very last breaths," he said, softer than I'd ever heard.

"So," I said, curling my lips into a smirk, "you're going to help me."

Carve drew his fingers across his blades, a spark inside him that he hadn't ignited for decades suddenly burning. Since King Xorgor had ascended the demon throne, Carve had been aching for another war. I could see it in his fucking eyes.

He tried to be smarter and wiser, but he had been cursed to fight.

"We're terrible friends," Carve said, which meant he had my back. No matter what.

"The fucking worst."

ZURI

"ARE YOU COMFORTABLE NOW?" Stone asked on our walk back to the pack house.

Chewing on the inside of my cheek, I stared down at the dirt path and debated on what I should say to him. I didn't know how much I could push him until he snapped, and I wasn't sure I wanted to test it, seeing that he had friends who liked to throw damn knives in our direction. I still couldn't get over the fact that Stone had grabbed the silver knife in his palm like it was nothing.

Nothing!

The last time I had touched silver, my hand had burned for weeks. And Stone had brushed it off like it was an everyday occurrence, his hand healing in a matter of minutes. I had never seen an injury heal that quickly before in my pack. We took at least a week to heal from the slightest touch of silver.

My pack had always spoken as if Alpha Stone were a devil, but maybe he was *the* Devil.

"You're giving me the silent treatment now?" he asked.

"No," I said quietly.

"Then, what is it?"

"Just thinking about today," I said, thoughts drifting to the massage and shopping. Nobody had ever spoiled me like that before, and I had never thought *anyone* would, especially not Stone. "Thank you."

"For what?"

"For bringing me out to town and not being embarrassed to be seen with me." The words slipped out of my mouth before I could stop them. I snapped my lips closed and wondered where the hell that had even come from. I had been thinking about how *sweet* the devil had been to me today.

Not that.

He growled and suddenly plastered me to the nearest tree, his callous hand wrapped tightly around my throat and his golden gaze piercing into mine. "Why the fuck would I be embarrassed to be seen with you?"

I sucked in a breath. "I-I didn't mean—"

"You fucking said it," he snarled, running his thumb across my lower lip. "Look at me."

With a trembling gaze, I peered up at him and wondered what he'd do to me. The last time I had mentioned my insecurities, he had forced me to stare into the mirror as he fucked me senseless from behind. Now, we were in public.

"Take it back," he growled.

"Or what?"

Fuck! What is wrong with me?! Why can't I keep my mouth closed today?!

He pinned his hips against mine, his cock hard on my stomach. I whimpered and pressed my thighs together, heat coursing through my core. He trailed his fingers up the column of my neck, strumming them.

"You want to be a brat for me, *mate*?" he asked.

Before I could stop him, he ripped off my panties from underneath one of the more conservative dresses he had bought for me today and lifted me into the air, placing my legs on either of his shoulders with his mouth between them.

I grasped his muscular shoulders to steady myself. "Wh-what are you—"

His tongue found my clit almost immediately.

I laced my hands into his hair and cried out softly, brow furrowed. "Y-you should put me down before you—"

"Don't speak," he growled, his voice vibrating my cunt. "Come."

And almost immediately, my body jerked in the air. He continued to massage my clit with his tongue, dragging it in circles around the sensitive bud as my wolf continued to enjoy her mate's touch.

He slipped one finger inside me, then another and another. I arched my back, the pressure building higher, and I gripped his hair tightly, a low moan escaping my lips once I finally relaxed in his arms.

"Good girl," he murmured, the praise sending me over the edge.

I threw my head back and cried out, riding his fingers and his face. He buried his tongue deeper between my pussy lips and sucked on my clit, driving me higher and higher for a moment, and then finally, I slowly came down from the high.

"That wasn't hard, was it?" he taunted.

"You can put me d-down n-now," I murmured, closing my eyes.

Still holding me in the air, he pulled me off his shoulders and dropped me right down onto his cock.

I widened my eyes and cried out, "Wh-what are you doing?!"

"Fucking my mate," he growled, slamming his hips up.

He drove himself into me over and over, pounding my pussy until I was quivering around him. Heat exploded through my core, and I gripped his muscular shoulders tightly, squeezing my eyes closed as the pressure rose quickly inside me again.

His mouth found my breast, and while this dress was semi-conservative, he still gained access to my tits through the neckline, sucking on the flesh he could find and slapping my ass like a wild, roguish animal.

"You're mine," he growled. "And I'll have you how you are."

"B-but—"

"So, stop fucking saying shit like that, *mate*, because it pisses me off."

I clenched around him and moaned softly.

"Do you understand?"

"Y-yes."

"Louder."

"Yes."

He pumped into me, slamming his cock so deep that it hit my cervix. "You're mine."

"Yours," I cried. "I'm yours!"

Almost instantly, he stilled inside me and grunted. I went to slap a hand over my mouth to muffle my moans, but he snatched it up so I'd scream out into the dark forest instead. Wave after wave of pleasure crashed through me, and I curled my toes.

His cock pulsed inside me, and then he finally pulled out and set me down.

"Stone!" an older woman called from deep in the forest. "Is that you?"

While Stone leaned back against the tree next to me to catch his breath, his biceps glistening with sweat as his chest rose and fell quickly, I scrambled to cover all my bits.

"Who is that?!" I asked frantically.

With a smirk plastered across his face, he chuckled. "My grandma."

"Your grandma?! What the hell is she doing out here?"

"We're on our property," he said nonchalantly.

"We're what?!" I exclaimed. Though I hadn't missed the way he said *our* instead of *his*.

He kicked himself off the tree and seized my hand. "Come on. We're going to meet the pack."

STONE

"STONE, LET ME SHOWER," Zuri said, tugging on my arm.

"No."

"But your cum is—"

"Buried inside you?" I finished, a smirk tugging at my lips. As far as I knew, Zuri hated the thought of carrying our pup. But it would happen. Soon. "Good. My pack will be happy, knowing that the next heir to the pack will be growing in your belly."

"Stone!" she scolded. Yet she didn't show any sign of refusal, like she had this morning.

The mate bond was doing its thing.

"We're not even mated yet," she hummed, crossing her arms. "Don't say that."

I seized the back of her throat, twirled her around, and gazed down at those huge fucking eyes and that bare neck, my canines lengthening. "So, if I marked you, then I can put a baby inside you right now?"

"Stone," she scolded again, placing her hands on my chest and glaring up at me, "no."

My gaze locked on to her neck, and I pushed some hair behind her ear to give myself a better view of it. Adrenaline rushed through my system, my canines extending even longer and aching to be inside her flesh.

"Zuri," I purred.

She sucked in a breath, her gaze flickering down to my teeth. "N-no."

"You don't want my mark?"

"That's not what I … I said," she murmured, her canines peeking out from under her lips.

A low growl escaped my mouth, and I drew my thumb across the tip of her teeth. "Mine."

She sucked in a sharp breath and gently bit down on my thumb with her canine, brows drawn together and those eyes—those fucking eyes—wide in anticipation. "You can't bite me," she whispered. "Not now."

I dipped my thumb between her lips. "I'll do what I want with you."

My wolf slowly grabbed power from me, pulling me away from all sense of control I had over myself, like he had the other night when we burned Zuri's workplace to the ground and left no survivors.

Her cunt salivated at my words from her pleasure, my wolf immediately picking up on her arousal. She sucked my thumb into her mouth like the pretty little mate she was and gazed up at me, as if she didn't have control either.

When she dropped her gaze to my throat, I lost it and slammed her up against the tree, our bodies pressed together and my face buried into the crook of her neck. I drew my canines up and down the column of her throat, gently sucking on the skin to prepare it for a mark.

For *my* mark.

"Little mate, I'm going to—"

"Stone!" my grandmother shouted again from the party.

After tensing, Zuri shoved her hands against my chest. I stumbled back and shook my head to regain control from my wolf, forcing myself not to bite her. She didn't want it, and while I hoped it wasn't because of her insecurities, I wasn't about to give her more.

One step at a fucking time, Stone.

Once she straightened herself out, Zuri turned toward the direction of my grandmother's voice and cleared her throat. "I guess we should get back to the pack then?" she suggested because, apparently, she would rather now meet my pack than have my mark.

Nodding, I guided her in the right direction.

"Please don't leave my side," Zuri whispered as we approached the pack house.

A bonfire raged in the backyard, the flames reaching the tops of the trees. A couple of warriors were bullshitting around it while their mates gossiped near the river. I wanted her to make friends here, and she wouldn't do that while glued to my hip.

"No promises."

"Stone, please," she said, staring up at me through huge eyes. "Not tonight."

"Fine," I said, grasping her hand. "I won't leave you."

She stayed tense for a few moments, and then she nodded. "Thank you."

When we stepped into the backyard, the girls from the river leaped up, hurried over to us, and grinned at Zuri before we could even make it to the bonfire. Zuri inched closer to me and intertwined our fingers.

"Hi!" Riley said. "Sapphire told us she met you earlier, and we were all so jealous."

"That's Riley," Samantha said from the group, pointing to each of them. "I'm Sammie. This is Jackson, Ruby, Georgie, and Naya. We're all mated to those *assholes* sitting by the fire, shit-talking to each other."

The women giggled, and my mate smiled along with them.

"It's nice to meet you all."

"You're probably going to meet many people tonight. If you forget any of our names, just ask. We'll be by the river all night, so you can stop over whenever you want to get away from the craziness," Georgie said.

Once Zuri nodded, they headed back to the river to gossip more.

I guided Zuri to the warriors near the fire to continue the night. For the first time since I had met her, she stayed glued to my side and barely said a few words, except some formalities, while the entire pack spoke to us.

And by the end of the night, Grandma Bee sat at the picnic table with a beer in her shaky hand. Zuri collapsed at the edge, blowing out a breath from meeting so many people, the tiredness etched onto her face.

"It's nice to meet you finally," Grandma Bee said. "I'm Stone's grandmother."

Zuri straightened her back and plastered a smile on her face. "Oh, sorry. I—"

"Don't worry about it, dear. You must be so tired." She turned to me. "Why'd you make her meet the pack all in one night? And right after you brought her home from her old pack? She must be exhausted."

Zuri arched a brow and shot me that *see, I told you* look.

"You know how it is," I said, sitting beside Zuri.

"You alphas," she said, shaking her head. "Can't control yourselves. Your grandpa was the same way. Always wanting to show me off." She leaned closer to Zuri. "Believe it or not, I was a sexpot back in my day, just like you."

Zuri's cheeks flushed. "Oh, I'm not—"

A growl escaped my lips, shutting my mate's insecurities right up.

Grandma Bee looked at me. "Now, as for you, I've been meaning to talk with you."

"What is it?"

She grabbed my hand. "You have a mate now. You should forget about all this nonsense, Stoney. Your mother's death was a hard one, but we have all moved past it. You need to protect those close to you."

"I'm not over it," I growled.

"Over what?" Zuri asked.

"Nothing," I said.

"He wants to … *take care* … of his father and brother. I'm sure he's mentioned them to you," Grandma Bee said.

"He's mentioned Dirt," Zuri said.

Grandma glanced over at me. "Dirt?"

My canines lengthened. "That's what that piece of shit is."

"Don't get all angry now," she hummed, clasping her beer tighter. "I miss your mom, too, but there is nothing we can do about it. Your father and brother are some of the strongest people in the world."

"They used that strength to humiliate, rape, and murder my mother."

Zuri tensed next to me, gripping my biceps a bit tighter. "T-that's horrible."

"What's horrible is that nobody has said a fucking word about it," I snarled.

After it had happened, they had continued to live out their lives like my father wouldn't do the same to anyone else that he had done to his fated mate.

This pack that I led wasn't my own. I wasn't really supposed to be alpha.

But that was too complicated to explain to my dear Zuri, and I didn't want her to fear for her life here. My pack and I were the only people who would actually protect her in this damn world. This pack and these people cared.

Unlike the people my father and brother led.

"Do you think—" Zuri started, a howl from deep in the woods cutting her off.

"Can't be a pack meeting without me," someone said from the forest.

I snapped up and growled. *Fuck.*

"Brother," Derrit said, stepping out from the darkness, "I'm home."

CHAPTER
FIFTEEN

ZURI

"DERRIT IS YOUR BROTHER?" I whispered, stepping back and staring at the man I had seen many times before back at my old pack.

He had hung around the bar at the restaurant every night, had been my sister's crush, and had even … snuck into my bedroom more than once.

My throat dried, fear rushing right through my body. My sister had always had a thing for him, but he always ignored her. Always showed *me* the attention. Which made my sister hate me even more because she thought that I wanted him back. I never had, but he'd kept coming around.

Derrit glanced at me, his lips curling into a small smirk. I stepped behind Stone and sucked in a breath, attempting to make myself as small as possible so he wouldn't see me, so he wouldn't *say* anything to my mate.

"Zuri," Derrit murmured, "how've you been?"

A ferocious growl escaped Stone's mouth. "Get off my property."

"Settle down, brother," Derrit taunted. "I'm talking to my gi—"

Before Derrit could finish his sentence, Stone leaped forward. I snapped my hand around his wrist and yanked him back with as much strength as I could because I had seen Derrit fight before. I knew the chaos he was capable of.

Stone struggled against me, but I dug my heels into the ground to hold him in place.

"Don't listen to him, Stone," I whispered. "Don't give him what he wants."

"Don't lie to your mate, Zuri," Derrit said. "You know what you meant to me long ago."

"What is he talking about?" Stone growled through clenched teeth.

"Nothing," I said, heart pounding. "He's talking out of his ass."

Derrit moved closer to us and bellowed in laughter. "I know the whole family, brother. I would bet that she hasn't introduced you to everyone yet, hmm? Her sister. Her friends. And her pretty little pus—"

Stone ripped himself out of my grasp, leaped up, and shifted midair into his enormous black wolf. Tears spilled from my eyes, and I stumbled back into Stone's grandmother as cries escaped my mouth. Derrit would kill him.

While Stone was crazy, Derrit was a werewolf with warlock abilities. He had cast magic so dark that entire towns turned to dust when he stepped into them—which I guessed was another reason they referred to him as Dirt. He had made demons crawl out from the ground and beheaded the town's children. It had been a horrific mess.

And if Stone wasn't careful, he and his pack would suffer the same fate.

"Derrit," I cried, my knees buckling, "please don't hurt him. Please, Derrit!"

When Stone latched his canines into Derrit's chest, Derrit

shifted into his wolf. I stared in horror at the two wolves, my stomach twisting and bile rising in my throat.

Stone's grandmother grabbed my wrist. "Come on, sweetheart. Let's get you to safety."

But I couldn't move because something wasn't right.

Derrit wasn't using magic, was incredibly weak, and the wolf's fur coat was blond, but, like Stone, Derrit had a black coat. At least, that was what I remembered of him. Yet both the wolves moved so quickly that … maybe I was seeing things. Or maybe Stone was too blinded by rage.

"That's not Derrit," Grandma Bee said a moment later, her grip loosening.

I wasn't seeing things. This must've been some magic spell that Derrit had cast on a wolf.

"Stone!" I shouted through my tears. "Stop it! It's not your broth—"

Before I could stop him, Stone sank his canines into the wolf's throat and tore it right out of his body. Blood splashed everywhere and splattered onto my face. I ripped myself out of Grandma Bee's hold and sprinted to Stone, grabbing his wolf by the back and yanking him away from the wolf who was slowly shifting back into human form.

Stone quickly returned to his human form, standing on his two feet, and spit the throat out of his bloody mouth. Another growl escaped his throat, his eyes as black as night. But when the man began forming, realization crossed his face.

It wasn't Derrit. It was his own packmate.

CHAPTER
SIXTEEN

STONE

WYATT, my packmate and one of my strongest warriors, lay at my feet.

I parted my lips and stared at the man I had once called a brother on the battlefield. Wyatt, Carve, and I had been the strongest of friends in our warrior days years ago. We had fought side by side, and I had just killed him.

Shaking my head, I dropped to my knees. "No."

After pulling him into my arms, I growled. Fucking Derrit and his magic. He had done this. He must have done this. I didn't know how, and I didn't know fucking why he had chosen now, but I didn't care anymore.

I would kill him.

The crowd collecting around us parted, and Wyatt's mate appeared.

"No," she cried, falling in front of me and yanking him away from me. "No!"

Her screams echoed through the forest, giving me shivers. I couldn't believe that I had killed one of my old packmates. That fucker wanted me to be exactly like him, wanted my pack to believe that I had done this willingly so they wouldn't trust me.

"I didn't mean—"

"I know," she cried, shoulders bucking back and forth. "I saw Derrit too."

While I didn't know what else to say—because I was still in shock myself—I stayed there with her and the rest of my pack-mates until she finally stood with him in her arms and walked to the river, asking for privacy.

I clenched my jaw to hold back the sorrow rushing through me, stood, and grabbed Zuri's hand. She followed me through the pack and back to the house.

"Derrit knows you," I growled.

Zuri gulped and stared up at me through teary eyes. "Stone ..."

"How does he know you?"

"It's a long story," she whispered.

"I have time."

She stopped, shifted uncomfortably from foot to foot, and tore her gaze from mine, chewing on the inside of her cheek. "He used to come around my old pack all the time and flirt with me ... sorta. At least, my sister said it was flirting. I just thought he was being nice."

Fury rushed through my veins, and I wanted to wrap my hand around his fucking throat and snap it. I hoped that she wouldn't be as naive, especially with him.

"Derrit isn't nice to anyone unless he wants to fuck them. Did you sleep with him?"

Just the words leaving my mouth felt like venom.

"Stone, come on," she whispered.

"Did you fucking sleep with him?" I roared.

"No," she said, shaking her head. "Of course I didn't. He tried to get me to sleep with him multiple times and even ... even attempted to"—she paused for a moment and glanced down at the dirt underneath her feet—"come onto me, but my sister walked into the room."

Tears welled in her eyes and ran down her cheeks. And when she collapsed onto the ground in a hysterical, sobbing mess, I dropped everything for her and took her into my arms. She curled into me, grasping my shirt and crying.

"I'm sorry. I'm so sorry. I never wanted to even touch anyone before I found my mate," she cried. "I wanted my first everything to be with you, and that was ruined by him. He stole my first kiss and my first …" She hiccuped and couldn't finish her sentence.

And honestly, I wasn't even fucking sure if I *wanted* to know what had happened. Once she told me, my wolf would take control and force us to find him now, kill him now. We wouldn't think clearly, and we'd get our entire pack killed.

"It's okay," I whispered, holding my wolf back. "You don't have to tell me."

"I'm sorry." She sniffled. "I'm sorry. I'm sorry. I'm sorry. I'm sorry."

Swiping my fingers into her hair, I gently massaged the top of her head. "Stop it."

I walked with her into the pack house, up the stairs, and to our bedroom, not wanting anyone—especially Derrit, wherever he was—to hear her cries of pain.

Once she finally calmed down, she lifted her head from my shoulder, stared up at me, and whispered, "Do you hate me?"

After setting her on the bed, I gently cupped her chin in my hand. "I could never."

"But I—"

"I. Could. Never," I repeated.

She pressed her lips together and swallowed hard, nodding softly. "I'm s—"

Before she could finish her sentence, I snapped her pretty mouth closed. "Stop apologizing for something that you haven't done, especially willingly. You're my mate and the luna of this pack. You need to be strong and confident in yourself."

"That's not who I am," she whispered.

"Yes, it is."

"No, it's not."

"You're stronger than any she-wolf in my pack," I said.

"You're just saying that."

"You were able to hold me back the first time I was about to attack Derrit," I said, honestly never having felt that strength and that power before. If she worked on becoming stronger both mentally and physically, she'd be taking *me* on soon.

I sank to my knees in front of her, my body between her legs and my arms on her thighs. "You're stronger than you even imagine, Zuri. And one day, you're going to have to come to terms with that. Do you understand me?" I asked, cupping her jaw. "It might not be today, but someday soon."

Because soon, she would have to lead this pack while I went to war against Derrit. She needed to be strong for the wolves who stayed behind, for the children who would lose parents and loved ones, and for the family that I would give her before I left.

CHAPTER
SEVENTEEN

ZURI

THE NEXT DAY, I stood somewhere in the forest that surrounded Durnbone with Maxine, Sina, Carve, and Stone. The guys chatted tensely with each other a ways away from us, Carve juggling his knives.

"I'm still so confused," I whispered. "Are Stone and Carve really brothers?"

Sina furrowed her brow and glanced over at me. "Who said that?"

"Stone called Carve his brother the other day," I said, watching Stone and Carve have the most intense conversation that I had seen.

Stone clenched his sharp jaw and shook his head, hands balled into fists.

"As far as I know, they aren't brothers," Maxine said. "Warriors who train and fight in battle together sometimes call each other that around here. And I think Carve fought alongside Stone in battle years ago."

"Yeah," Sina agreed. "I don't know Stone well, but I thought he only had one brother."

"Derrit?"

Maxine grimaced. "Derrit. Dirt. Same thing. Same person."

"You both don't like him either?" I asked.

"I used to work at the tavern downtown, and he would … visit a couple of years ago." She shivered and looked toward the guys. "More than once, I had to close while he was still at the bar, drinking."

Sina frowned. "From what I gathered, my mates don't like him either. Especially Darius."

"Darius?" Maxine questioned. "But he's so nice. What did Derrit do to him?"

She shrugged. "I don't know. He seemed pissed when Carve was talking to them last night about the coming war …" She glanced over at me. "And about what happened yesterday. That must've been so terrifying for you."

My lips curled into a frown. "Stone was more shaken up about killing his own packmate than I was about seeing Derrit. I used to work at a restaurant, and Derrit would come in throughout the week." My stomach turned. "He always gave me the creeps too."

More than the creeps, but I didn't want to admit that to Maxine and Sina yet.

"All right," Carve said, walking over to us while flipping a knife. "Ready?"

"Ready for what?" I asked, peering at Stone, who leaned against a tree.

"To train," Stone said.

Eyes widening, I snapped my gaze between the two war buddies. "Here? Now?"

"Yes," Stone said. "I already told you that you'd be training."

"Don't worry," Maxine said with a smile, backing up. "You'll have fun."

A knife whizzed by me, barely grazing my ear. I screamed and ducked, holding my arms over my head to protect myself and squeezing my eyes closed. I would much prefer to fight as a wolf than have knives thrown at me!

"Fun?!" I exclaimed, dodging another knife that nicked my finger.

"Catch it," Stone ordered, heading toward me.

I picked the blade up from the dirt and gripped it in my non-wounded hand.

"Apologies that I'm not a psychopath like you!" I snarled at him, licking the blood off my finger. It might've been just a graze, but I didn't heal as quickly as Stone's ass did. My wounds sometimes took hours to heal.

Stone grabbed my finger and drew his tongue across my wound, his dark gaze never leaving mine once. When he pulled my finger from his mouth, he smirked, that dark hunger in his eyes, like the first night we had met.

"There," he hummed as if it wasn't anything.

When I peered down at my finger, my eyes widened. The wound was completely closed.

"Do you have magic too?" I asked, brow furrowing. "Like your brother?"

"No, I heal quickly because—"

Carve nearly snorted. "Because he made a pact with a devil."

"Carve," Stone growled.

"A deal with a devil?" I repeated. Looking at Maxine, I asked, "Someone like your mate?"

"No," Stone answered. "Xorgor is an incubus. The devil that I made a pact with was a demon, skilled in fire. He's long dead now, but some of his abilities still run through my veins. They come in handy."

My eyes widened slightly, and I tried to remember why Derrit had told me that he had magic. If they both came from a family of warlocks, then Stone should have magic too—or at least *some* magic—right?

"And your brother?" I asked. "How'd he get his?"

Carve and Stone glanced at each other, and then Carve cleared his throat. Another blade whizzed through the air.

"Stone?!" I leaped back and stared at Stone in horror. "You're really going to let him do this to me?"

"Time to train, babe," he purred.

So, for the next three hours—yes, three!—I ran away from Carve's knives, Maxine's demon attacks, and Sina's ... well, I wasn't quite sure *what* kind of species she was or what her attacks were, but she was so strong.

And then I ended up attempting to fight my mate once they all left.

"Get up," Stone ordered, his hips pinning mine to the ground.

I placed both hands on the dirt and attempted to push him off me, but my arms gave out, and I landed on my chest. He pressed his backside against mine once more and took a fistful of hair in his left hand.

"Up."

Using all my strength, I pushed myself to my hands and knees.

But within a second, he scooped his arms underneath mine and collapsed them, flipped me over onto my back, and then slipped between my legs. He dipped his head so his lips grazed mine, his warm breath fanning my face.

"I said to get up, mate," he murmured, drawing the prick of his claws up my side and to my breast. He squeezed my tit and grunted, "Can't let an alpha like me take advantage of the vulnerable position that I've put you in."

CHAPTER
EIGHTEEN

STONE

"GET OFF ME," Zuri growled, shoving her hands against my chest, the heat of her cunt warming the front of my pants. She slammed her fists into my shoulders in a weak attempt to move me off her.

"You can do better than that," I said.

She was playing with me now, but I didn't blame her. She had spent all day fighting Carve, Sina, and Maxine, and now, she was facing *me*. And I wasn't about to let her off easy, like everyone else had.

"Fight me."

"I can't!" she said. "Your dick is pressing against my pussy."

"Don't let that distract you."

For a moment, she dropped her hands and glared up at me. "You're an ass—"

I dipped my head and pressed my lips against hers. She inhaled sharply, her fingers now curling into my muscular chest and her body relaxing against mine. I ground my hips further against hers and growled into her mouth.

"I could've killed you in eighteen different ways during our kiss," I mumbled against her lips. "Stop getting distracted and fight me back, mate. I know you're stronger than this. You wouldn't let anyone plow into you like me, would you?"

She growled, "Don't even say that."

After taking one of her hands, I placed it against the bulge in my pants. "Fight. Back."

She stroked my dick through my pants as I pushed against her cunt.

"Don't let me make you come just from this," I murmured. "Fight me."

She scooched her hips back, but as she did so, I slipped my fingers around the waistband of her pants and pulled them off her. She sucked in a sharp breath, whimpering slightly, and reached down for her leggings.

I tore her pants apart with my claws and then fondled her wet cunt with my hand. She punched me straight in the jaw, sending me back a couple of inches, and scrambled to her feet, smirking down at me.

"Serves you—"

A ferocious growl left my throat, and before she could say another word, I shot to my feet and sprinted toward her. She widened her eyes and turned on her heel, running straight through the forest, half-naked.

"S-Stone!" she shrieked. "I didn't mean to hurt you!"

While she ran quicker than I had ever seen, I allowed her to make it a few more feet into the forest before I captured her by the waist, twirled her around, and pulled her into the air. She grasped on to me, about to say some shit about how I should put her down, but I would have none of it, especially now.

"Sit on my cock, mate," I purred, losing my pants and slamming myself deep into her hole.

She wrapped her trembling legs around me and whimpered in pleasure, her pussy squeezing around me. Grunting, I picked her up off me and dropped her on my dick again. And again. And again.

She seized my chin in one hand and a fistful of my hair in another, pulling my head back and staring down at me. "I hate you," she growled, then kissed me hard on the mouth, sucking my tongue ring between her lips.

My dick swelled at the sensation. "How much?"

"So fucking much."

I wrapped my arms underneath her arms and grabbed her shoulders, pounding her down onto me and getting as deep as I could inside her warm pussy. "Cute," I purred into her mouth. "Is that why you're about to come for me?"

After growling into my mouth, she yanked back my hair again. "I am not."

"Getting feisty with me now? Are you finally ready to fight me, mate?"

"No, I'm—"

Before she could finish her sentence, I pounded up into her so hard that I hit her cervix. She cried out—and I wasn't sure if it was in pleasure or in pain—and gripped my shoulders.

"I'm not going to come," she growled. "I'm not going to come. I'm not going to—"

I pressed the head of my cock against her cervix, my cum spewing out into her cunt and hopefully getting her pregnant this time. So much of my cum pumped out of me that it filled her up and began running down her thighs.

"Only thing that matters to me is getting you pregnant with my pups," I said.

Though she mattered more to me than that. But I wanted her to tip over the edge.

And like I had planned, she threw her head back and screamed in pleasure.

CHAPTER
NINETEEN

STONE

ONCE I BROUGHT Zuri back to our pack house to rest, I walked alone to Wyatt's house to check in on his mate after last night. She had requested privacy to heal from her mate dying in my hands, but I needed to make sure she was okay.

Guilt rushed through me. After everything that had happened with my father and brother, I'd vowed to protect my packmates from anything. And then I—tears built in my eyes—had killed one of the men who had trusted me the most.

After knocking on her door twice with no answer, I rocked back on my heels and promised myself that I wouldn't break down in front of anyone today. I had done this with my own two hands. I had to pay the consequences.

The distinct stench of blood drifted through my nostrils, and I tensed. *The fuck is that?*

When I didn't get an answer after the third knock, I broke the lock on the door and followed the smell of blood to their bedroom. I knocked—for decency—and yet again didn't receive an answer, so I opened the door and nearly hurled at the stench.

Wyatt's mate lay in a puddle of her own blood with a pregnancy test in her hand.

My stomach dropped, and I immediately scooped her up into my arms and sprinted toward the pack house, heart racing. I didn't know what she had used, but the slits on her wrists were inches deep. She had cut multiple veins and blood vessels and wasn't healing.

"What happened?!" a doctor exclaimed.

I placed her into his arms and shook my head. "I found her like this at her home."

"We'll take care of her, Alpha," a nurse said, ushering the doctor into another room.

"Keep her alive," I said, chest tightening. "Please."

"You should get cleaned up," Riley said, grabbing my wrist and bringing me to the bathroom. "Luna Zuri won't want you coming home all bloody." She ran some water in the sink and washed off the blood of Wyatt's mate. "How is she doing after last night?"

"Okay," I said, mind numb.

What had happened to Wyatt's mate? After last night, she seemed ... okay. I mean, much better than she did today. She had never been the type to ... to think about even doing something like this, but ... maybe the pregnancy test had thrown her off.

"She's having a pup," I whispered.

"Zuri is?!" Riley exclaimed.

"No, Wyatt's mate."

Zuri didn't want my pups, not yet.

And while it killed me on the inside, I had to respect her wishes.

———

"Fuck," I whispered, sitting on the edge of our bed and running a hand through my hair.

Zuri glanced over her shoulder at me and frowned. "What's wrong?"

"Nothing," I said, refusing to turn around now and let her see me like this. "Go to bed."

After a moment, the bed shifted, and Zuri's arms came around my shoulders. "We might not be mated yet, but I can feel your emotions, Stone. You're an asshole most of the time, but you don't usually feel like this."

"I'm fine," I said, running another hand through my hair.

I didn't want to tell her because I didn't want her to think I wouldn't—or couldn't—protect her from my brother. But I couldn't get over the fact or the thought that he had made it through my borders and corrupted one of my good friends. I couldn't believe that I had *killed* one of my best and closest warriors because I thought it was him.

"I visited Wyatt's mate tonight to see how she was doing," I admitted.

"And?"

"And I found her in a puddle of her own blood," I whispered, my entire body tightening and tears building in my eyes. I balled my hands into tight fists, letting my claws sink into my palms. "She was holding a positive pregnancy test."

"Oh my Goddess," she whispered, pulling me closer. "Stone, I'm so sorry."

"It's fine," I mumbled, though my heart was crumbling.

My pack would be torn apart because of my actions. The doctors were working on keeping her alive as we spoke, and I … I was here, about to cry in front of the one person I had sworn to protect.

"I don't know if she'll live," I whispered, clutching on to her elbow.

When Zuri's arms tightened around me, I opened my mouth and let out a sob. While she had been vulnerable in front of me way more than once, I had never wanted her to see this side of me. I wanted her to be confident that I would protect her at all costs.

Because she needed it.

She didn't think that she was strong or that she deserved love.

"I'm so sorry," she whispered. "Both of you must be going through so much pain. This doesn't compare, but I remember when my mother died when I was just a child. I felt so much hurt that I wanted to … to do that too."

"No," I said, a low growl leaving my throat. I whipped my body toward her and shook my head. "Don't fucking say that, Zuri."

She swallowed hard. "I don't want to now, but the thought crossed my mind. She was my rock and the only person who ever truly cared about me. It's hard when the person you love the most is torn from you."

"Is that why you don't want to get close to me?" I asked.

She stiffened and pressed her lips together, not saying a word.

"Zuri," I whispered, the tears and stress building in my eyes. "Is that why you don't want to mate with me, why you continue to refuse wanting to mate me or to have my pups? Because I'm not going to leave you."

"Life is so precious," she whispered. "You don't know what will happen."

"The Moon Goddess won't let it."

"That's what all wolves believe," she said.

"That's what I know. There's something different about us. About *you*."

I didn't know what it was, but I could feel it in my bones. We were mates, but Zuri was one of the most powerful women I had ever met. Not only on the outside, but on the inside too. And she was sweet—almost too sweet.

She had more love than hatred for her sister who had bullied her. She hadn't wanted me to kill any one of the people who had made her life miserable because she loved life. And now … now, I knew why.

Still, Zuri was different. I truly believed that. One day, I'd prove it to her.

But for now, the only thing I could do was love her.

CHAPTER
TWENTY

ZURI

I STARED up at the bland ceiling through wide eyes. Darkness blanketed the room as Stone snored lightly beside me. I glanced over at his bare, scarred back and pressed my thighs together, heat gushing through me.

My body and my wolf were slowly betraying my every last wish. From the moment I'd laid my eyes on the madman, I hadn't wanted to mate with him. Never mind have his pups! But the thought of him loving me so much that he wanted me pregnant …

"Fuck," I whispered, squeezing my legs and eyes closed.

How could I even let this thought cross my mind? I hated him so much, but … he was actually so sweet. He acted all tough and hard in front of his pack, in front of other wolves. He was feared by almost every other pack that I knew.

Yet still, tonight, he had cried in front of me while thinking about his packmate that he had killed. He hadn't forced himself upon me, like his brother had tried. He had pampered me the other day, bought me clothes that I actually looked decent in and, for the first time ever, that I felt ... sexy in. And don't get me started on that dirty mouth of his.

But what I liked the most was ... I didn't feel insecure around him as much anymore.

Though that fear, those insecurities, still lingered sometimes, and I sat up late at night, wondering why the hell he was with me and why the hell I was enjoying it. I shouldn't feel like this, especially after the bad news that he had brought home to me last night.

"Curse you, Moon Goddess," I whispered.

She hummed to me, like she usually did late at night when nobody else was around. "He's good for you, my daughter," she said, her voice like harmonies during the new moon when she wasn't even in the sky, glowing bright. "I promise."

"He brought me my family's ashes."

"They'd deserved it."

My eyes widened, and I sat up in the bed as she came into existence near the window. She sat on the windowsill, a small smile on her brown face and her eyes glowing white, and kicked her legs back and forth.

"What do you mean, they'd deserved it?" I asked. "Aren't you supposed to love—"

"Everyone equally?" She laughed. "Not when they're assholes."

"Stone is an asshole."

"You think that man, who was sobbing in your arms tonight, is an asshole?" She arched her brow, giving me that infamous *who are you kidding* look that Mom used to give me before she died when I was only a child.

"But he—"

"He's your fated mate for a reason," she said. "You need him as much as he needs you."

"He's an asshole!"

"Is it that you really think he's an asshole or that you don't think you deserve him?"

I chewed on my inner cheek. "I just don't get it sometimes. How is he attracted to—"

"Don't you dare finish that sentence," she said, leaning back on her arms. "Do you see my body? I'm not skinny or muscular or traditionally beautiful, like most wolves are. Yet still, they worship me. Not because of my appearance, but because of my heart."

"But you are beautiful," I said. "Truly."

She shook her head. "You should let Stone fuck you in front of the mirror more often. Maybe you'll start to see what I see and what Stone sees. True beauty lies on the inside, but you, my dear, are beautiful, both on the inside and out."

"Did you watch us?!" I asked in horror.

"No."

I narrowed my eyes. "You did."

"I did not." She giggled. "I promise. But if you don't start believing in yourself, you won't be able to protect this pack."

My mouth dried. "Protect it from what?"

"From what's coming."

"Which is … Derrit?"

She paused and looked away. "I've tried to stop him with my own power, but I can't."

"You can't …"

"But you can."

"Me?" I whispered.

"Or, you know, I can *make* you."

"And how will you do that?" I asked. "I'm not strong. We're not mated."

She smirked. "I can put you through heat. Force you to mate."

"You would not put me through heat right now."

"Your choice."

"Heat doesn't happen until the full moon."

"Heat happens when I say it happens."

"B-but—"

She hopped off the windowsill and stalked toward the bed.

"You know you want him." She laid a hand on my mate's shoulder, and while she was the Moon Goddess, the gesture still made me possessive. "Look at him."

I pressed my lips together and refused to respond because jealousy would drip from my voice like venom.

She stroked his hair. "Do you think he'd want to—"

"Get your hands off my mate," I growled.

Almost as quickly as she'd laid her hand on his head, she pulled it away and smirked at me. "There's my girl." She walked back to the windowsill and slipped onto it. "Now, all you have to do is let him mark you."

"Let him mark me?" I repeated the words quietly to myself, glancing down at my mate.

The Moon Goddess lifted her fingers, and a gust of warmth blew through the room, searing my neck. I sucked in a sharp breath as the warmth grew hotter and hotter, almost to the point where it became unbearable.

From the focal point, heat radiated through my body. I pressed my thighs together.

"What have you done to me?" I asked.

"Helped you along."

Heat gushed between my legs, and I lay back in the bed and closed my eyes, vowing that I wouldn't wake Stone up—because if I did, then I feared I'd say something *terrible* to him. And by terrible, I didn't mean something that I didn't actually want.

Because I wanted him to mark me. To claim me. To give me his pups.

The thought rolled through my mind again, and I sucked in a sharp breath.

"The thought of having his pups excites you, doesn't it?" she muttered.

"No. No. No. No. No. No. No," I whispered.

"Who are you talking to?" Stone murmured, turning toward me.

I stared at him through wide eyes, then at the disappearing

outline of the Moon Goddess, who was fading behind him. She threw me one last smirk, and with a whisk, she vanished into the form of a flickering candle on our nightstand.

Stone snapped his head in the direction of the sudden flame. "Did you—"

Before I could stop myself, I gently took his chin in my hand, turned his head toward me, and pressed my lips against his. The intense heat suddenly flared. He stiffened for a mere moment, then melted into the kiss, his arms slowly snaking around my wide hips.

"Zuri," he said between kisses, "what's going on? Your eyes … they're glowing. I've—"

"Put a pup inside me."

CHAPTER
TWENTY-ONE

ZURI

"WHAT?" Stone asked, almost in disbelief.

I paused for a moment, desperately trying to fight the deepest urges inside me. "I—"

Just as I was about to speak the words that I hadn't meant what I said, a sudden heat rushed through my body. I turned toward him, my hand on his taut chest and my nails lengthening into claws, digging into the thick muscle.

"Put a pup inside me," I cried.

While he had told me many times over that was exactly what he wanted to do, he gently grabbed my hand. "Are you okay? It must be sixty degrees in this room, and you're sweating. What's going on—"

Before he could speak another word, I ripped the bedsheets off our bodies and straddled his waist, immediately feeling some relief when my pussy brushed against his hard cock. I closed my eyes and focused on the sensation.

"Zuri, I don't think—"

"The heat," I muttered. "The heat is gone like this."

"Heat?" he repeated, his canines extending past his lips.

"You're not supposed to go through heat for another couple of weeks, until the full moon." He grasped my waist harder, as if his control was slipping as well, and pinned my hips against his. "Does that feel good, my little mate?"

I whimpered slightly, "I need you inside me."

Hesitation washed through his eyes for a moment. "Is this what *you* really want?"

"Yes," I cried, panting on top of him.

Heat rolled down my spine, spreading through my limbs to my fingertips. I squeezed my eyes closed, wanting to slip into an ice-cold bath, but I knew that cursed Moon Goddess wouldn't even let my heat go away then.

"No," he murmured, as if he could read my mind. "It's not."

"It is," I begged, attempting to wiggle my hips and slip his cock inside me. "Please."

A low growl escaped his throat, his wolf attempting to escape Stone's cold, hard grasp on the situation. I howled low, needing him to rescue me, to fuck me, to use me and mark me and take me as his.

"Please," I cried, the pain unbearable. "Put a pup inside me."

"No," he said again, this time much stronger.

"If you loved me, you'd do it," I said. And then immediately regretted my words because they were wrong. Manipulative. But I couldn't talk straight anymore. My wolf ached more than she ever had, my entire body burning up in pain.

Suddenly, Stone flipped us over and pinned my hands above my head, his eyes a golden yellow. "Don't you ever fucking say that again. You know I would do anything for you, but you're not in the right mind, and I'm not going to fuck you while you're like this."

"B-but," I whimpered, on the verge of tears, "I'm hurting. Badly. Please, help me."

Somehow. Someway. I didn't care how he did it, but I couldn't do it myself. The only ease I felt was skin-on-skin contact with him; the only coolness right now was against my wrists. I tried grinding up into him, but he pulled his hips away.

And then he dipped his head and kissed me softly on the mouth.

Not hungrily, like I had been. Not ruthlessly, like usual.

"Relax," he whispered against my lips. "I'll give you a pup when you're ready."

"Stone," I whimpered.

He slithered two fingers down my chest, between my breasts, and then to my pussy. I immediately relaxed against the bedsheets, wanting more, but the pain was not as intense. He moved his fingers around my clit in small circles.

"If you're a good girl and stay just like this, maybe I'll let you come," he said.

I stared up into those glowing golden eyes and clenched, the pressure rising.

"Would you like that?" he asked.

"Yes," I said breathlessly. "Yes, please."

"Be a good mate for me," he said, burying his face into the crook of my neck, his teeth gliding up and down the column of my throat and making me shiver in the midst of heat. "And maybe I'll give you more than just an orgasm."

I tilted my head to the side to give him room, heart pounding. "Please, mark me."

This wasn't even my wolf talking anymore. The heat had subsided substantially. And I was thinking in my right mind for once tonight. After the Moon Goddess had talked to me, something had clicked—that wasn't my heat.

"Do *you* want it?" he asked. "Not your wolf. *You*?"

"Yes," I breathed out. "I do—"

Before I could finish the sentence, Stone plunged his teeth inside me. It was so sudden and so unexpected. I hadn't thought he would actually do it, but pleasure soared through my body, driving me higher and higher as an orgasm tipped me over the edge.

I screamed and cried and clawed up his back in an attempt to displace all the ecstasy surging through me. My toes curled, and I moaned into his ear, my canines lengthening too. I drew my teeth against his bare neck, my body on the clouds but weak.

Too taken by the pleasure to move anymore.

And so I lay there in his arms with my teeth millimeters from his neck and his mouth sucking gently on the mark he had left on me. My body still trembled, but I grasped tightly on to his shoulders, bringing him closer.

"Goddess," I whispered, "I love you."

CHAPTER
TWENTY-TWO

STONE

"I LOVE YOU TOO," I murmured back to Zuri so naturally.

I didn't know if she had meant it. She had been too deep in the pleasure from my mark. But I didn't care either way because I knew exactly what she meant to me, and now, we would forever be together.

She wore my mark.

After a couple of quiet seconds, Zuri stopped trembling and closed her eyes.

I turned onto my side and draped my arm around her waist. "Who were you talking to earlier?" I asked, tucking some coily brown hair behind her pierced ear with small golden studs and wondering why the hell the Moon Goddess had given *me* a goddess as a mate.

She paused, then glanced over at me while still lying on her back, her lips curled into a soft and satisfied smile and her eyes still glimmering how they had been during her heat. "The Moon Goddess."

"The Moon Goddess?" I repeated, furrowing my brow and wondering if this pack and I were making her crazy.

Sometimes, I cursed the Moon Goddess out for what my brother and father had done to us, but she had sounded like she was having an entire conversation with her.

"Yeah," she said. "I haven't seen her in a while."

"What do you mean?"

After shifting onto her side and scanning my face, she frowned. "I usually see her every week, at least once, which is probably not a lot, compared to you, but I appreciate all the time I have with her."

"You see her?" I asked. "Like … visually?"

Another quiet moment passed.

"Yes …"

"For how long?"

"Since I was a child. Why?"

"I don't see her," I said. "And I don't know anyone else who does."

"Oh, come on." Zuri playfully pushed my shoulder. "You're lying. Everyone sees her."

My fingers curled into her wide hips as I attempted to close my mind around this … thought. "The Moon Goddess has never even shown up to me in a dream, and you were straight-up having a real-life conversation with her, Z."

"Z?" She giggled softly.

The sound was so soft, so harmonic that I almost didn't believe it was coming from her. Because for as long as I had known her—which wasn't too long—she had always pushed me away or *tried* to.

Tonight, she was different. And I didn't know whether it really was because of the conversation with the Moon Goddess or not, but either way, I could do nothing but thank her for everything she had given me in the past few weeks.

For my mate.

"You're different tonight," I whispered. "What'd she say to you?"

Zuri paused. "I told her that you were an asshole."

My lips dropped into a frown. "Am I really that bad?"

While she didn't respond right away, her gaze lowered to my tattooed chest, and she curled her fingers into the muscle. "No," she whispered. "You're not really that bad. For so long and sometimes even now—and you know this—I think I … I don't deserve you."

"How many fucking times do I have to tell you that you're beauti—"

"That's not what it is about," she murmured. "At least not all the time." She leaned forward and rested her forehead against mine, a tear slipping down her cheek. "My sister, my family, and my pack bullied me for so long because I … I wasn't like them. I talked to the Moon Goddess a lot, and people thought I was just talking to myself. They told me that I would never find a mate, and if I did, he'd think I was weird too. And from there, it got worse." She tensed in my arms and pulled me closer, tears spilling down her cheeks. "So much worse."

I wrapped my arm around her waist and drew her to my chest, brushing her tears off her cheeks as they fell. "You don't have to tell me about it if it's too hard," I whispered, chest tightening. "I don't want you to cry."

"I want you to understand," she said. "I've always wanted a mate and tried so hard to be … normal. I was as nice as I could be to everyone in my pack and my family, hoping that, one day, they would see that I was just like them. I loved them all so much that I didn't realize how hard they actually were on me. And when you came along … when you killed them …" She shook her head. "I don't know. I felt so much hatred for you but so much less anxiety. It was weird. I didn't—and still don't—know how I felt about it. And all your compliments are so foreign to me. I don't know how to take them."

"Zuri," I whispered.

Because I honestly didn't know what to say to my own mate. It was obvious that her packmates had bullied her, but I had thought it was because of the way she looked. Because, fuck, that was why *I* had gotten so many tattoos—to cover up the blotchy red patches of birthmark left on my skin and the scars my fucking father had given me when I was younger because of them.

"You're one of us now," I said, gently taking her chin in my hand. "You're accepted here."

"I'm afraid," she admitted, "that, one day, you'll think I'm weird, too, for talking to myself, or not being as strong as a true luna can be, or if we have a pup, she'll experience the same things that I have, and I won't be able to protect her."

"Nobody is going to bully you or our pups. Not in this pack."

"What if they do?"

"I'll turn them to dust and give you their ashes. Over and over and over again."

"Stone, you can't do that," she said.

"Watch me."

She gave me that *are you serious* look, then playfully smiled and swiped at my shoulder. After a second, she bit back a smirk and looked away from me. "You know, the Moon Goddess also told me that you should fuck me in front of the mirror more often."

I chuckled and pulled her on top of me. "Is that right?"

Another laugh escaped her mouth. "Maybe …"

An easy silence drifted upon us, but I didn't want to push my luck and breed her tonight.

"When I was a kid, my grandma used to force me to sit in front of the mirror and tell her what I liked about myself," I whispered, staring up at her. "I hated it so fucking much at first, but I learned to love it, and you will too."

For the first time, Zuri relaxed on top of me and smiled. "Why'd she have you do that?"

I paused. "The full story will take a while to explain."

"Well"—she smiled—"we have some time before the Moon Goddess bestows another bout of heat upon me again. Tell me all about it, Stone. About your childhood, your pack, and your father and your brother. I want to know all about you, *mate*."

CHAPTER
TWENTY-THREE

STONE

WHILE I HAD PROMISED Zuri that I would tell her everything, as soon as she turned toward me to give me all of her attention, the words seemed to stick in my throat. I snapped my mouth closed and sighed softly, scooting to the end of the bed and dropping my feet to the floor.

"Do you see my tattoos back here?" I asked, drawing my fingers across my back.

The bed dipped behind me, Zuri inches away from me on the mattress. She drew her fingers across the tattoos on my back, the skin that I had hated for years of my life.

"Yes," she whispered. "What about them?"

"They cover up a birthmark that spans from shoulder blade to shoulder blade."

"A birthmark?" she repeated. "Why would you cover that up?"

"Because it's disgusting."

"Stone, how do you know it's disgusting?" she asked. "You can't even see it."

I pressed my lips together. "Because it is red and blotchy and huge."

"And?"

All this time, I had been telling Zuri not to worry about what other people thought about her, that their opinions didn't matter. Yet, I had been the biggest hypocrite in existence. I had let my father's and brother's opinion make me hate my skin.

"And ..." I whispered. "Derrit and my father would hurt me for it."

Zuri sucked in a small breath, then moved closer to me until she sat flush against my left hip. She moved her fingers across my back, right over the birthmark that I had hated forever and ever. For fucking years.

"How would they hurt you?" she whispered, her mouth against my shoulder.

Kissing the ruined skin.

Once her lips lingered there for a few moments, she finally pulled away and glanced over at me, her eyes burning with such intensity that I thought I was sitting next to the Moon Goddess herself right now.

Truthfully, I had wished that the Moon Goddess had visited me when I was younger, when my father and brother would beat the living shit out of me every night until I had enough of it. Until I left their rule with some of the others that I now call packmates.

"What did they do to you?" she asked again.

I leaned back on my right palm and drew my fingers over the claw marks across my rib cage. "My father did this to me when I was four," I whispered, the pain shooting through my body at the memory.

Tears filled her eyes. "Stone, this looks like it was deep."

"It was," I murmured. "I didn't think I would make it. I remember lying in a pool of my own blood at the doorstep of the pack house. My father's business partners came over that night and stepped over my dying fucking body without even asking if I needed help. They didn't care."

My throat closed, and I balled my hands into fists.

"H-how'd you … survive?"

"My grandma finally found me," I said. "And from that moment on, I lived with her."

"Still with your pack?"

"It was never my pack," I said. "Derrit is older and the first-born son of the alpha. If I hadn't left before he became alpha at eighteen, then he would've killed me on the spot to make sure that nobody would challenge him."

She leaned her head on my shoulder and drew her fingers across my scars again. I didn't have many scars anymore since I had made the deal with that devil, but I had been too young to heal these scars.

I hadn't even shifted for the first time when they happened.

"How'd you end up here?" she asked. "With your grandma and your pack?"

"After we left, I traveled around a lot. Joined wars and battles to become stronger. Trained with Carve and Wyatt. Most of the people in this pack are misfits too, coming from slaughtered families or running away from home."

Her lips curled into a small smile. "You created a home for people like … me."

"For people like *us*," I whispered, turning toward her and resting my forehead on hers.

Suddenly, James's voice drifted through my mind link. I paused for a moment, listening to his words.

"Wyatt's mate is alive, but we have a problem. Derrit and your father have just raided a pack nearby. Word is that they're traveling with all their warriors. Here."

I ran a hand through my unruly hair, kissed Zuri, and slipped off the bed. "I'll be back later, mate. I have business to take care of and a pack to protect. My father is on his way here. And we need to prepare."

"Before you go," she said, grasping my hand, "I'd like to have a girls' day with Sina and Maxine sometime soon."

My lips curled into a smile. "I'll arrange it for you then."

CHAPTER
TWENTY-FOUR

ZURI

"DON'T HOLD BACK," I said to Sina.

We stood in the backyard to her pack house with Maxine. I had told Stone that I wanted to have a girls' day—which surprised him, but he hadn't asked questions. Honestly, I wanted to get stronger for him.

After Stone had told me everything that had happened and why he had become the Stone that I knew today, I wanted to protect him. I hadn't known him for that long—and had thought that I hated him for the time I *did* know him—but I felt like I knew him now.

We were the same. Both bullied by the people who were supposed to love us.

Except my packmates were dead, thanks to him. And his family was still alive.

Sina transformed into a half-werewolf, half-monster, throwing attacks my way that I could just barely dodge. Part of me believed that she was still holding back, but at least she was harder on me today than the other day.

There was no way that I would ever be as strong as Sina,

Maxine, Carve, or even Stone. But I would try to become stronger and stronger to protect the pack of misfits and runaways. I was now their luna, the woman they looked up to.

In the middle of an attack, Maxine hurled a knife in my direction and caught me in the arm. I fell to the ground and yanked the blade from my flesh, the blood oozing out between my fingers. Maxine and Sina hurried over.

Sina pressed her hand to the wound in my upper arm, her eyes glowing and the wound instantly closing. I still wasn't exactly sure what kind of creature Sina was, but she was more than the average werewolf.

"Thank you," I said, dusting myself off. "Both of you."

Maxine smiled softly. "Sorry for your arm. I didn't mean—"

"It's okay," I finished. "I want to get stronger."

"I think that's enough for today," Sina said.

"Me too."

"Do you wanna go to the Dead Candle Tavern with us?" Sina asked.

Maxine curled her arm around her best friend's. "Olenna will be there."

"Who's Olenna?" I asked.

Maxine and Sina grinned at each other, and then Maxine turned back to me. "The girl we're trying to set Carve up with. They were lovers in many, many, many past lives, but they're enemies in this one. It's kinda funny and cute."

"She legit hates him. Carve acts like he hates her too." Sina giggled. "But he doesn't."

"Yeah, Carve has the ability to refresh time," Maxine said, pulling me down the path toward Durnbone. "Rumor has it—at least, this is what I heard from Xorgor—that Carve has refreshed time over a thousand times to find one life where Olenna doesn't die."

My eyes widened. "Holy crap. He can do that?"

"He is the strongest warlock to ever walk in this world," Sina said, nodding.

"But he acts like a grumpy old man most days," Maxine said. "Come on. She's probably waiting for us."

———

"There is no way," I said, laughing when we stepped into the Dead Candle Tavern.

Olenna was the smallest, cutest, most innocent thing ever. I wanted to just squeeze her until she popped—*hello, cute aggression*. But I couldn't even wrap my head around how someone like her would ever be with Carve, who was just as crazy as Stone.

She laughed softly. "What?"

"You like Carve?"

"What?!" Olenna fake gagged. "Who told you that?"

I glanced over at Sina and Maxine, who hid their smiles behind their glasses of ale. Olenna arched a brow at them, a hundred thousand emotions flooding through her system. Then, she finally sipped her drink and shook her head.

"I hate him now, and I will always hate him."

"Suuuure," Sina said, cheeks reddening from the alcohol.

"It's true!" Olenna exclaimed. "He's a terrible person."

"He didn't seem *that* bad," I added. "Except for … his weird obsession with knives."

"He has literally burned entire towns to the ground, has killed innocent people, and is desperate to make my life a living fucking hell," she growled. "I have barely seen him throughout the years, but I still feel his eerie presence all around me."

"Eerie presence?" Maxine asked, sniffing. "Smells like horniness to me."

"Don't use your demon abilities on me," Olenna said. "And it is not horniness."

Sina and Maxine shared another look, and I could tell another drawn-out *suuuure* was lingering on Sina's lips. I bit back a laugh, not sure if this was how friend groups formed or even if I was part of their friend group yet.

I had never once been out to a bar with girls to have fun before.

Stone would be proud of me when I told him.

Suddenly, the entire tavern quieted down to a whisper.

"Oh," Sina said. "I hope you don't mind. I invited the guys."

"The guys?"

I glanced over my shoulder to see four wolves, one demon, Stone, and the one and only Carve waltzing into the Dead Candle Tavern together, all serious-like, talking about—I assumed—war plans.

Olenna sipped her drink. "As long as Carve isn't here, then I'm—"

"You have got to be fucking kidding me," Carve growled, stopping halfway to our table.

Olenna snapped her head in his direction, her eyes blazing with hatred. "What is he doing here?" she said between gritted teeth, her fingers whitening on the tabletop and her human teeth bared to him.

Sina threw an arm around her shoulders and pulled her closer. "Oh, you know … they're here to talk about war plans. Wanna stay?"

"No! I don't want to stay," Olenna said, snatching her belongings and hopping up.

She stormed toward the exit, passing Carve on the way, who then turned around and followed her right out of the tavern.

Maxine hummed, "Ah, to have lived a thousand lives and still be in love."

STONE

ONCE WE FINISHED at the Dead Candle Tavern with everyone and anyone who was someone from Durnbone, I ran a warm bath for Zuri and me. I had to meet with Thayer, Carve, and Xorgor a bit later to finalize some plans for the next few weeks, but I wanted to spend time with my mate.

I pulled my shirt over my head and tossed it into the hamper. Zuri peered into the bathroom, her gaze falling to the tub, filled with water and bubbles.

She stepped into the room beside me and smiled. "What's this for?"

"Relaxing," I said.

She giggled. "You relax in a bubble bath?"

"You don't?"

After laughing behind her hand, she shook her head. "Not usually. I just can't picture you"—her gaze drifted to the tub, then back to me—"relaxing in a bathtub, filled to the brim with bubbles. You seem more like a bloodbath kind of guy."

"And you seem like the kind of girl who had better get her ass into that tub with me before I strip off all her clothes myself and toss her in there," I hummed, a smirk playing at the corners of my lips, my wolf aching to get out and have her already.

Since I had marked her earlier this morning, I hadn't been able to stop thinking about her. She had been gone nearly all day with Sina and Maxine, which made me happy, but that mark had been taunting my wolf.

Zuri fiddled with the buttons on her shirt, then pulled it off her shoulders. So agonizingly slowly. I slipped off my pants and stepped into the bathtub, slouching down into it and letting the warm water soothe my muscles.

Once she pushed off her pants, she followed my lead. Halfway to sitting down, she paused and glanced over at me, eyes wide. "Wait … this doesn't have my family's ashes, does it?"

A chuckle escaped my lips. "No."

"Why do I not believe you?" she asked.

"I swear on the Moon Goddess."

After narrowing her eyes at me even more, she finally sank down into the bubbles with me and leaned her head back against the edge, sighing softly and smiling to herself. "Guess what."

"What?"

She bit back a smile. "I think I have real friends."

Warmth spread through my chest, and I shifted in the water to wrap my arms around her waist and pull her into my lap. Water sloshed over the edge of the tub, but I couldn't find it in me to care about it.

"I'm so proud of you," I murmured.

While she had been trying to hide her smile, a wide grin stretched across her face. She set her hands on my round shoulders and curled them around the muscle. "We spent all morning together training and then—"

"You were training?" I asked, shocked.

Cheeks reddening and rounding, she nodded. "I wanted to surprise you. I think I'm getting stronger by just a little bit. Maxine and Sina are very good at fighting, so I wanted to practice with them to be a good luna for this pack."

My chest tightened, and now, *I* couldn't hide my smile. "You were training for us?"

She nodded and drew her hands across my chest muscles. "Only because of you. If you hadn't pushed me endlessly to become a better version of myself, to push away my insecurities, then I never would've even thought about it."

"That's not true."

"Yes, it is," she whispered and rested her head against mine. "I love you, Stone."

ZURI

AFTER STONE BATHED WITH ME—*YES, my big, bad mate bathed in a bubble bath*—he helped me into one of the robes that he had bought me the other day down in Durnbone. I smoothed it out with my fingers and stared into the full-length mirror at him behind me.

For a while, I hadn't known what had come over me last night when I practically begged him to put a pup inside me. But now, I did. I hadn't gone crazy. I hadn't let the Moon Goddess affect me with that heat.

I had been in my right mind.

"Is there a reason you're drooling?" Stone asked, arching a brow at me.

Biting back a smile, I peered at my mark in the mirror. "Just admiring my mate."

"Don't start with me," he growled. "Or I'll cancel my meeting tonight to—"

"Put a pup inside me?" I asked, lifting my gaze to his in the mirror again.

Another growl escaped his lips. "You'd better watch that pretty mouth of yours."

"Or what?"

He moved closer to me, his large hand grasping the back of my neck and his tongue on the mark he had left on my skin. He flicked it, his tongue ring making me warm in all the right places. "Or I *will* put a pup inside you tonight."

I twirled around, my lips curled into a small smirk. "Good."

"Where has the soft, scared, *hates everything about me* Zuri gone?" he asked me.

"She's"—I paused, my voice barely above a whisper—"fallen for you."

Once he snatched my chin in his hand, he drew me toward him and pressed his lips against mine. "I'll be back. James is here," Stone said, snaking his arms around my waist and pulling me closer to him. "Don't let anyone else into the house, okay? According to our scouts, Derrit is making his way closer to here."

"Okay." I nodded, gently patting his chest. "I'm not going to let your psycho brother in."

After letting out a low chuckle, he kissed me on the lips and then disappeared out of our bedroom door and into the hallway. A couple of moments later, the front door clicked closed. I fell back on the bed with my arms sprawled out and sighed.

I wished that Derrit weren't coming at all. I didn't want to see him or deal with him. I had had enough of him when I was back at my old pack, but it seemed like everything was about to get a lot more—

"Zuri." A whistle drifted through the bedroom.

Heart racing, I snapped up to a seated position and glanced around the room.

"Oh, Zuri," Derrit murmured, his voice like the wind.

My fingers curled around the bedsheets until I gripped them tightly in both my fists. I swallowed hard and squeezed my eyes closed, knowing that this was another one of his mind games. Somehow, someway, he had slithered into my head.

And when Stone returned, I needed to tell him.

"My sweet girl." The voice came again. "So precious."

"Stop it," I growled, slapping myself in the temple with the heel of my palm. "Stop it!"

"So cute, thinking that I'm inside your mind," he said. "I'm so much closer than that."

I jerked my head to the side, glancing over my right shoulder in an attempt to spot him. And in the darkness, I swore that I saw those devilish eyes staring back at me. I jumped up from the bed and backed up until I hit the door.

"Get away from me!" I screamed, grabbing the lamp and hurling it in the bed's direction.

When it crashed against the wall and shattered, I snapped out of the trance he had put on me and blinked a couple of times. He wasn't here. He wasn't in the room, behind the bed, or in the closet.

"Zuri!" James called from down the hallway, his footsteps quick. "What's going on?"

"I-I'm fine!" I shouted.

"Zuri," he said again, the tone of his voice dropping, becoming lower, morphing into Derrit's. "Zuri, what's going on? Zuri, are you okay? Zuri, what was that noise I just heard? Zuri. Zuri. Zuri. Zuri. Zu—"

"Stop it!" I screamed at the top of my lungs.

The door behind me rumbled, but I dug my heels into the ground so Derrit couldn't barge into the room and hurt me. Tears welled up in my eyes because I hadn't been strong enough to hold him away, to push him out of my thoughts.

I tried. I really did.

"Open up, Zuri," Derrit said again, a dark chuckle escaping his mouth. He pounded on the door behind me with his fists. Taunting me. "Open up, Zuri. And let me in the same way you've let Stone in. I want to be inside you."

As the words left his mouth, the door busted open and off the hinges, sending me flying forward onto my stomach. My arms felt so weak, but I scrambled to my knees and crawled as quickly as I could to the window.

"Get out of my head!" I cried, tears streaming down my cheeks.

"You're not strong enough to be a luna," Derrit said behind me, his hands on my shoulders. "And you know it. A luna wouldn't be crawling in a pitiful attempt to escape. She would be—"

I grabbed a piece of the shattered lamp and swung it backward, slashing it across his face. When blood spewed everywhere and Derrit stumbled backward, grasping his face, I turned around and backed up to the wall.

My vision began clearing, and I realized that it wasn't Derrit, but James.

Hands trembling, I dropped the glass. "I-I-I'm s-sorry. I'm sorry, James. I didn't—"

When he pulled his hand away from his face, the wound had already healed, and his face contorted back into Derrit's. My fingers shook because I didn't know what was real anymore. Was this really Derrit pretending to be James? Or had Derrit taken over James's body?

"D-don't move any closer," I said, snatching the bloody shard and pointing it at him.

"Zuri," he taunted, hands up in surrender, "you got me."

"You're a prick!" I said through gritted teeth, my hand shaking. "Get away from me!"

Suddenly, Stone hurried in from behind Derrit, his eyes wild and his canines lengthened. He scanned the room, his gaze landing on the man in front of me. And then he hurried past him and scooped me into his strong arms.

"D-D-Derrit," I said through hiccups, pointing at the man. "I-It's h-him."

"It's okay, baby. I'm here." Stone pulled me to his chest. "I'm here to protect you."

TWENTY-SEVEN

ZURI

AFTER SNIFFLING into Stone's chest for the last hour, I finally crawled off him and wiped my tearstained cheeks. I hiccuped and bit my lip to hold back another sob. I hated feeling so weak. I had just finished telling Stone how strong I was getting.

Then, I had gone and almost killed his beta.

"Wh-where is James?" I asked between sniffles.

"Out in the kitchen," Stone said, reaching for my hand. "Why don't you rest?"

"I need to see him," I whispered.

Instead of placing my hand in his, I walked to the bedroom door as tears stung my eyes. Part of me hoped that nobody else in the pack knew about what I had done because I didn't want them to hate me. I needed them to trust me, but I didn't even know if I trusted myself around anyone other than Stone now.

I pulled open the door and stepped out into the hallway of the eerily quiet pack house, and then I glanced over my shoulder to look back at Stone. I reached out my hand again. "Please, come with me. I don't trust myself to be alone with anyone else."

Stone hopped up from the ground, where he had been holding me, and took my hand in his larger one, intertwining our fingers and squeezing. I gently tugged him down the hallway toward the kitchen with my stomach in tight knots.

"Do you think he'll forgive me?" I asked, brow furrowed.

"Yes."

"B-but I almost killed him."

"He will understand that it was Derrit," Stone said.

When we reached the kitchen, I peeked around the doorway and glanced into the room to see James standing by the sink with his hands on the counter, gazing out the window and into the forest. My stomach twisted into knots. I wasn't sure if I even wanted to see his face.

My mind was shot, and I could barely remember how much I had hurt him.

"J-James?" I whispered.

Stone gently squeezed my hand.

James twisted his head and gazed back at me with a small smile on his face. "Luna—"

My lips parted, and I released Stone's hand, walking toward James in astonishment. His face and all his wounds were completely healed, and he was … smiling at me.

Why was he smiling at me after I had almost killed him?

If I had done that in my old pack …

"I'm sorry," I whispered, drawing my fingers across his cheek, where I was almost certain that I had cut him. "You're healed already. I … I'm sorry. It should've never happened. I can't believe I hurt you."

"It's okay, Luna," he said. "I'm glad you're feeling better."

Tears trembled in my eyes. "It's not okay."

"Yes, it is," Stone said. "He understands that it was Derrit."

Lips curled into a frown, I glanced over my shoulder at my mate. While they were both saying that it didn't matter, it did matter to me. I had hurt someone, like my sister and family and ex-pack had done to me many times.

I had done the one thing that I'd vowed *never* to do.

"You don't have to worry about me," James said, chuckling. "We've seen worse."

"Come," Stone said, capturing my hand and pulling me toward the door. "You need rest."

After triple-checking to make sure James was okay, I followed Stone back into the bedroom and crawled into bed.

He tucked me in like I was a child and kissed me gently on the lips. "If you feel like that again, call for me. I will be in the other room. Understand?"

I nodded.

Once he left, I closed my eyes and tried to rest. But my mind buzzed.

"You let Derrit in," the Moon Goddess whispered, her voice drifting like the wind.

"I hadn't meant to," I said, clutching the sheets to my chest. "I really hadn't—"

"Shh, shh, shh," she cooed. "I know you hadn't meant to, but you have to resist. You know what his power feels like now. And in order to protect your pack and your mate, you must refuse to let him in like that ever again. Fight his control."

Guilt rushed through me. "I'll try."

"You must, dear Zuri. Now, close your eyes," the Moon Goddess said, swiping her fingers from my forehead to my nose so I would flutter my lids closed. "I want to show you something. I need you to focus on Derrit."

"I don't want to let the thought of him slip back into my mind," I whispered. "Please."

"One time," she murmured. "I promise, he can't hurt you."

After squeezing my eyes shut, I furrowed my brow and blew out a deep breath. My stomach twisted into knots as I lay back on the bed and tried to relax so I could think semi-clearly. I didn't know what she was about to do, but I trusted her.

And if something happened, Stone was in the other room. He'd save me.

"If you don't stop Derrit, this is what Durnbone will become," she said.

Suddenly, fire burned around me, blazing as tall as the buildings in downtown Durnbone. Stone crumbled from the buildings and turned into dust. Pups were taken from their home, forced into slavery. Young girls, barely even teenagers, were raped by the men in Derrit's pack.

Tears burned my eyes, and I shook my head. "No, this can't be true."

"But it will be, dear Zuri, if you don't stop it."

I opened my mouth to question, but I lowered my gaze and saw Stone's head at my feet, his eyes open, his skin pale, and his blood draining from where his neck should've been, creating a pool of gooey liquid underneath my bare feet.

"No," I cried, dropping to my knees and grasping his face. "M-m-my mate."

"Don't let Derrit win," she whispered. "I can't stop him myself."

"Tell me how to stop him," I said, wiping my tears with the back of my hand. I reopened my eyes and gazed up at the Moon Goddess, who stood next to me with her fingers intertwined. "Tell me what I need to do. How can I stop him?"

"You're the only one who knows how to stop him," the Moon Goddess said, placing her hand on my shoulder. "I cannot tell you what to do. I can only guide you in what I think is the best direction."

"And what is that?"

When I closed my eyes again, the image of what Durnbone *could be* disappeared, and I saw Derrit and his warriors setting up camp about three miles south of Durnbone. Which meant that we didn't have much time left. They had traveled so quickly.

Almost *too* quickly as a pack.

"T-they're that close?" I asked, mouth drying.

"Yes, my dear."

I balled my hands into fists by my sides and gritted my teeth, glaring at him in my vision through tears.

We had to stop him. Tonight.

TWENTY-EIGHT

STONE

"STONE!" Zuri shouted from the bedroom.

After leaping up from my office chair, I hurried past the other warriors that I had called in for a meeting and ran straight out of the room to find my mate. She had barely been resting for thirty minutes. If that fucker had—

"Stone!" she said, zipping through the hallway toward my office. "We have to go."

"Where—"

Before I could even get out a word, she grabbed my wrist and continued toward the back door. I dug my heels into the ground and stopped right at my office, catching Zuri's wrist and leading her into the room with the other wolves.

"We have to go," she repeated, a bead of sweat rolling down her forehead.

"You have to rest," I said.

"If we don't—" She inhaled sharply, her gaze falling to my neck and her lips quivering. "If we don't go now, then everything … we'll …" Another rapid breath. "We're all going to die. He'll kill everyone in Durnbone. I saw it."

"Who?" James said.

"Derrit," she said, hyperventilating now.

I placed my hands on her shoulders and drew my thumb across her mark. She relaxed her shoulders just a bit, her body still tense. She stared up at me through teary eyes, lips quivering hard.

"You have to believe me. I spoke to the Moon Goddess."

"The Moon Goddess?" one of my warriors whispered. "When?"

"Just now."

"Are you sure it was her?" James asked Zuri.

"I'm positive."

"How do we know this isn't one of Derrit's games?" James asked.

I believed that Zuri had seen the Moon Goddess. She had seen her while I slept in the room the other night, but I ... I wasn't sure what to think right now. What if it had been a dream to help Zuri through this? What if it really had been Derrit messing with her still?

"I've seen the Moon Goddess many times throughout my life," Zuri said.

"I know you have," I said to my mate, loathing the fact that part of me didn't believe that this was the Moon Goddess. "But do you think it is a coincidence that she came back again after Derrit visited you?"

Zuri dropped her gaze, tears trembling in her eyes. "I-I don't know."

The warriors began chatting skeptically among themselves about Zuri's visions of the Moon Goddess. As far as I knew, nobody in my pack had ever had visions of the Moon Goddess similar to hers, and I didn't want Zuri to think they were poking fun at her.

Or worse, didn't believe her.

But we couldn't run into things, especially with Derrit.

"Either way," Zuri said, balling my shirt in her fists, "we have to do something."

"Why don't we sleep on it? We have warriors posted every half-mile around our borders," I reasoned with my mate. "Then, tomorrow morning, I will call a meeting with the packs around Durnbone, and we can talk."

"It will be too late," Zuri whispered.

"Too late for what?"

"Y-you're going to die," she cried, collapsing to her knees and shaking her head. "I saw it, Stone. He decapitated you. Your head was at my feet. Durnbone was in flames, crumbling, turning to dust. Girls were … girls were being raped. Boys taken as slaves …"

"Fuck," James murmured from the other side of the room, running a hand through his messy hair. He looked up at me and spoke through the mind link. *"If what she's saying is true, then it's just like the prophecy said."*

"Derrit hasn't even made it halfway to Durnbone yet," I said.

She wrapped her arms around herself. "You're wrong. T-they're already here."

"What do you mean?" I asked. "Our spies said—"

"Alpha," one of my warriors, Calr, said through the mind link, *"we spotted—"*

Suddenly, the mind link ended, my thoughts to Calr empty, which meant that …

James sprinted to the back door, shifted into his wolf, and ran into the forest, where Calr had been stationed tonight. Zuri sat in tears at my feet, grasping on to my thigh, like if she didn't, then I would disappear.

"You have to believe me," she whispered. "If we don't stop him tonight, then Derrit will kill us all."

TWENTY-NINE

ZURI

"WE NEED A PLAN," I said, hurrying after all the warrior wolves racing out of the house.

Stone rushed by me and headed for the back door, growling to himself. I ran up to him, grabbed his wrist, and dug my heels into the ground. If they ran out to Derrit blindly, then it would be even worse.

"Stone," I attempted to reason, "please, you have to be careful."

"We will."

"You don't know what he's capable of," I whispered.

Twirling around, Stone stopped at the back door. "*You* haven't seen what I'm capable of."

My eyes widened slightly, brow furrowing. I … he was right. I didn't know what he was capable of, but I had seen what Derrit could do with his own magic. As far as I knew, Stone didn't possess any kind of magic. At least none like that.

"You're staying here," Stone growled at me.

His eyes burned black, his canines dripped with thick saliva, and his claws extended far past where I had ever seen them. I hadn't seen him this pissed since he'd brought me home and then gone back to my old pack to burn it to the ground.

Tears welled up in my eyes, but I refused to back down. "You're not leaving me alone."

After snarling at me, he turned toward the door. "Don't leave my side and stay shifted."

And then he leaped into the air, transformed into his large black wolf, and ran into the forest. I followed in his footsteps, shifting into my wolf and running after him, pushing myself so fast to catch up to him.

Halfway to the borders, he glanced over his shoulder at me. *"Don't fall behind."*

"We should go to his camp," I said through the mind link. *"This has to be a trap."*

"I'm going to murder him," Stone said, running faster.

"You need to outsmart him. Not out-magic or out-muscle him."

Wolves howled in the distance. I cursed underneath my breath and continued forward to catch up with Stone's large beast. Two enemy wolves lunged at me from the back left, and I barely even caught sight of them before Stone turned and ripped their throats from their bodies.

They smacked against the ground with a thud as blood dripped from Stone's canines. I jumped over Stone, spotting another wolf lunging toward us, and swiped my claws across his belly, so deep that his guts spilled out onto the ground.

"Protect my neck," Stone said. *"And I'll protect yours."*

Three more enemies ran at us from the north, and I swept my snout underneath my mate's neck while he lunged forward to fight the beasts. Adrenaline rushed through my system. My mind was focused on one thing: my mate.

A wolf reached under in an attempt to bite Stone in the throat, but I caught his snout between my canines and bit down so hard that I crushed his nose and jaw in the process. He howled out in pain as Stone finished him off by swiping his claws across his belly.

"When I tell you to run," Stone stated, *"you run."*

I howled in response. *"I'm not leaving you out here alone."*

Another two wolves lunged at us from behind. Stone whipped his tail so hard that after the impact, one flew through the air and smacked into a tree. The other caught my backside between his teeth, and I fell onto my belly and growled in pain.

A ferocious growl escaped Stone's mouth, and he sank his teeth into the wolf's neck, shattering every bone inside it until the wolf released his grip on me. And then Stone jumped on our enemy, tore each of his limbs off, and continued to rip him apart until patches of his fur littered the forest around us.

I scrambled to my feet and dipped my head underneath Stone's neck as the other wolf ran toward us from the tree. I snapped my mouth around his neck and tore out his throat to protect my mate.

Blood dribbled from my mouth and onto the leaves underneath my paws. Stone roared and spit out guts onto the ground, scanning the area for any other sign of enemy wolves or his own brother.

"There are too many of them. My packmates are dying. When I say to run, you run."

"And leave you here?" I exclaimed. "No."

"Unless you want to see me turn into the demon who burned down your old pack, run."

"I'm not going anywhere unless it's with you," I said. "If we die here, we die together."

A low growl escaped his throat. *"We won't die tonight."*

Fire suddenly blazed from his fingertips, engulfing his entire body. The man that was Stone was no more, and a demon stood in his place, taking over his body, flesh becoming burned charcoal and the whites of his eyes becoming black masses.

Trees were set aflame, creating a ring of fire around the fighting and corpses. It burned so heavily and so hot that any wolf who attempted to leap over the fire burned to dust within moments, their ashes drifting in the blazing breeze.

Sweat rolled down my back, yet I stood behind Stone and watched the enemies burn to pieces around us. I stared up at him, my heart pounding and my nipples taut. It wasn't the time or the place, but I had never seen such ... strength and power in my life.

And when all the enemies burned away in the madness, the fire died out within Stone's body. He stood before me, breathing heavily as pieces of his flesh burned with the flames. Part of me believed that we might really have a shot at beating Derrit.

That we could possibly win.

James stood over the enemy wolves, shaking his head.

"Find Derrit," Stone said to the remaining warriors. He walked over to James and placed a hand on his shoulder, squeezing gently. "You good—"

Before he could finish his sentence, James turned around and slammed his extended claws right into Stone's throat and hurled him halfway across the wooden landscape. "I'm right here, brother. You've already found me."

Blood gushed from Stone's mouth, and he collapsed onto the ground, his body transforming into his human. I shifted into my human and dropped to my knees, my hands on his wound to keep it closed so he wouldn't die.

"Stone," I whimpered, fingers shaking.

"R-run," he said, voice a hoarse whimper.

"I'm not going—"

"Run before he kills you too."

CHAPTER
THIRTY

ZURI

"I ALREADY TOLD you that I'm not going anywhere without you," I cried.

I stood up in front of my mate, vowing to protect him, no matter what. I had never seen someone fight with so much vigor, so much strength and intelligence, and *still* get defeated by a man who used other people's bodies to do his dirty work.

And while I had always feared Derrit and never stood up for myself before in front of him—or any of my family—tonight was different. I refused to watch this man kill my mate and do nothing about it.

"I'll kill you for hurting my mate," I snarled at James. "I'll kill you for good, Derrit!"

James, who was really Derrit, smirked at me. "I love women who put up a fight, baby. Come at me." Derrit stepped forward, his eyes blazing so many different mesmerizing colors. "Women like you taste better."

Stone stood to his feet, one hand pressed against his throat, and stumbled up to me. He grabbed my arm harshly and pushed me behind him, fire blazing from his fingertips and burning me. "I'm not going to tell you again. Run!"

Before I could push him out of the way, Derrit used his magic to control the trees, creating branches from his fingers and shooting one that must've been six inches thick through the air and into Stone's abdomen.

Pain shot through my body, and I screamed out in agony for him. I wanted to comfort him, but my wolf wouldn't let me. Instead, I lunged in Derrit's direction, one thought racing through my head.

Kill Derrit. Kill Derrit. Kill Derrit.

Derrit formed another thick, sharp branch and shot it at me. It pierced straight through the center of my chest, breaking my sternum. I grabbed the branch in my fist and yanked it from my flesh, then hurled it back at him.

"Stay away from my mate!" I screamed, my voice echoing through the forest.

The branch pierced his shoulder and set Derrit flying back against the nearest tree, pinning him to the trunk. Adrenaline rushed through my veins. I transformed into my wolf and sprinted at the man who had hurt my mate.

This might not truly be Derrit, but I needed to end his life.

My mate might die because of him.

Before I could reach his impaled body, he shot another branch in my direction, piercing my left thigh. I yanked that branch out of me and stabbed him directly in the chest. He grunted in pain, forming another branch.

A tree to my left shriveled up and crumbled to pieces near Stone. Derrit was using power from the trees, sucking out their magic and their life, just as he was doing to James right now. Which meant that I needed to get him out of there.

"Get out of his body!" I screamed, wrapping my hands around James's throat. "Now!"

The harder I squeezed, the brighter the skin on his face seemed to glow. He didn't deserve to live, but I refused to kill one of Stone's most trusted men because of his shitty brother. James wouldn't do this to me. To us.

Mesmerizing colors twisted in his eyes. He attempted to escape my grip, but I held him tighter and tighter and tighter, refusing to release him back into the world. Derrit wouldn't leave this pack alone, and I didn't care what I had to do to force him to stop.

"Get out!" I shrieked, shaking him back and forth. "Get out!"

A couple of moments passed, and the colors began fading from his eyes.

"Zuri," James whispered. "Z-Zur-ri, it's me."

But I didn't believe him.

"Zuri," Stone called from behind me, coughing, "it's James."

I dropped my hands from James's throat and glared at him, but he lifted his unharmed arm and pointed behind me at my mate.

"G-go help him. He's going to … die if you don't do something."

After twisting my head, I locked my gaze on my mate to see him on the ground with blood pooling out of his wounds. He held his hand to his chest, blood gushing between his fingers. I ran over to him and grabbed the piece of wood.

My body moved as if I had done this before, as if I knew exactly what I had to do to keep my mate alive. I didn't know what was going on because pulling a piece of *anything* from someone's body without proper medical equipment was against everything that I had learned.

But I yanked it from his chest and placed my hands against it.

Like James's face had, Stone's skin glowed as I touched him.

"We need pack doctors!" I shouted to the other members. "Someone!"

"We'll find someone," Sina said, disappearing with Maxine into the forest.

I hadn't seen or heard them prior to this very moment, but as I looked around, I spotted more warriors than were in Stone's pack. Four wolves to my left, beat up and bruised. Xorgor to my right, standing with Carve. They had come.

Stone coughed again and grabbed his chest, the blood thick between his fingers. "Zuri."

"We're going to get you help. Hold on."

"Look me in the eyes, Zuri."

"Stone, this can wait. You're bleeding out. We need to get you to—"

He grabbed my chin and forced me to look into his eyes. And in the reflection of his black pupils, I saw mine glowing a bright white against his darker ones, blazing as brightly as the Moon Goddess's eyes always did in my dreams.

"I told you," he whispered, his wound healing on its own now, "you are stronger than you realize."

CHAPTER
THIRTY-ONE

ZURI

MY GAZE DARTED between Stone's eyes and the wound healing quickly. Wh-what was happening? Why … why were my eyes glowing inside of his pupils? They were … white. Why were they white?!

"What's going on?" I whispered, hands shaking and mouth dry. "Why are my eyes—"

"Calm down," Stone said, his wound closing completely.

I opened and closed my mouth a handful of times, scrambling to my feet and slowly backing away from him. My heart raced, and I rubbed my eyes with the heels of my palms, hoping that it'd go away.

Stone pushed himself to his feet, gaze on me. "Zuri, you're okay."

Though my packmates whispered to each other, their voices rushing through my head loudly. There were so many voices that I couldn't even decipher any of them, except Stone's—which soothed me, only to an extent.

When Sina and Maxine finally returned with a doctor—who

didn't need to help Stone, but all his other warriors instead—Sina walked over to me, brow furrowed.

She lifted my chin with her fingers. "Let me see."

"No," I whispered, squeezing my eyes closed.

"Please."

After a deep breath, I finally lifted my gaze to meet hers. She squinted for a moment, as if she hadn't expected them to be so bright, then smiled softly. Maxine bounced over to us and gazed over her shoulder at me.

"Is she a Paragon?" Maxine whispered.

"A Paragon?" I repeated. "Wh-what's that?"

While I had heard of many species that resided in Durnbone, I had never heard of a Paragon. Granted, my old pack didn't have many books in our pack library, so I couldn't have known about them if there were many.

"I'm a Paragon," Sina said, pursing her lips. "I ... don't tell many people this, but I have powers almost as strong as a god. Though my species is a dying one right now. If there are more of us, we need to know."

"Have you ... noticed any powers? Any strengths?" Maxine asked.

"Like what?" I asked.

"Visions maybe?" Sina said.

"No."

"I thought that you saw the Moon Goddess," James—who I had almost killed—called.

I glanced over at him and gnawed on my inner cheek, spotting Stone helping his warriors to the medical center with Sina's mates and Maxine's mate. Sina gently tilted my chin back toward her.

"Is that true?" she asked.

"Yes."

"What kind of visions are they?"

I shrugged. "I see her and talk to her. Mostly through dreams."

"Daydreams?" she said, brow arched.

"Sometimes. Is that bad?"

After Sina released my chin, she frowned and looked at Maxine. "No, it's not bad. But I've never spoken to the Moon Goddess before, and I have visions. I can connect with other Paragons, too, though I can't seem to form a connection with you."

"Does that mean I'm not one?"

"I'm here! I'm here!" Olenna shouted from the edge of the woods. She leaned over her knees, breathing heavily, and waved with one arm. "Sorry I'm late to the party. But it seems like you took care of business all by yourselves."

"The fuck would you even contribute to a war, Olenna?" Carve growled.

She narrowed her glare at him and scowled. "I'm not here for you, so fuck off." Just as he was about to respond, Olenna slammed her open palm into his face and shoved him back with it. "Get lost, piece of shit."

When he finally grumbled and stormed off, Olenna turned back to us and widened her eyes when her gaze landed on me. "Holy … moly, what is going on with you? Why do your eyes look like that?"

"We don't know," Maxine said.

Sina sucked in her inner cheek. "I would just keep an eye on it. Seems like it's fading."

"Keep an eye on it?!" I exclaimed. "How am I supposed to do that if I can't even see it?"

Maxine snickered. "Good point."

Sina smiled and leaned her forearm on Maxine's shoulder. "I'm sure it will be easy for Stone to keep track for you. He's obsessed with you."

"Mesmerized," Olenna hummed, her gaze flickering over to Carve for a moment.

A burst of butterflies fluttered in my belly from the way they exchanged a quick glance.

"*You* can be mesmerized too," Maxine said to Olenna. "If you ever let Carve—"

Olenna pointed a finger at Maxine. "Hey. You finish that sentence, and I will personally cut off your mate's horn tonight in his sleep. And I know how much incubi use their horns to get off. Don't test me, Maxi."

Maxine giggled and bit back a smirk, as Stone returned.

"So, Stone," Sina said, glancing over my shoulder, "make sure you record when this happens with her eyes. What she's doing. The emotions flowing through her. Times of day. That sorta thing."

"Thank you for your input, but I can take care of my mate myself."

"Just looking out for her." Sina smiled. "She's one of us now."

"One of us?" I asked, wondering what she meant.

A Paragon? No. *A wolf?* I had always been one of those.

"One of the girls." She grinned.

Warmth exploded through my chest, and I bit back a giant grin that desperately wanted to cross my face. I had never ever had a group of friends, never mind a group of close girlfriends. I didn't want to scare them away already.

"We really have to come up with a name for us," Maxine said. "Now that there's four."

"Durnbone Deadly Quartet," Olenna offered.

"That sounds like an old-timey band," Carve said. "You're shit at picking names, Olenna."

Through gritted teeth, Olenna pushed out a breath, then marched right over to Carve. She pinched Carve's ear between her two nails and dragged him deep into the forest. Their argument drifted to us until their voices became more distant.

"Well, guess that's our cue to go," Maxine said, looping an arm around Sina's elbow.

Maxine pulled Sina back to their guys, and they waved over at Stone before disappearing through the forest too. Once we were completely alone, I finally slumped my shoulders forward and rested my head on the center of Stone's chest.

"You don't think anything bad is going to happen to me, do you?" I whispered.

"No."

"My eyes usually turn gold during a shift," I explained, like he hadn't seen them many times over. Still, I couldn't make sense of this at all. "They've never turned white before tonight. I don't know—"

"Nothing is going to happen." He gently took my face in his hands and swiped his thumb across my bottom lip until I parted them. Then, he slipped it into my mouth. "Besides, *my little mate*, I think it's sexy."

"Sexy?" I stared up at him, bewildered. "You're not worried?"

"No, but you should be worried."

"W-why?"

"Because if you don't make it home by the time I catch you, then I'm going to fuck you where I find you, *mate*." A low growl escaped his throat as his nails lengthened into claws. "So, you'd better start running."

CHAPTER
THIRTY-TWO

STONE

FOR A MOMENT, confusion crossed her face, but then she glanced down at my body transforming into my wolf, and she leaped into the air. Black fur sprouted from her body, and she took off through the forest.

We ran, and we ran, and we ran. And once I finally caught up to her, I shifted into my human. Then, I wrapped my arms around her waist, tossed her straight up into the air, and caught her with her thighs on my shoulders and her pretty little pussy against my mouth.

She transformed into her human, her giggles drifting through the dark forest around us. "S-Stone, wh-what are you doing?"

With my hands on her ass, I squeezed, buried my face even deeper between her thick thighs, and pressed my tongue to her folds. I flicked her clit with it and held her body steady as she jerked from the sudden pressure.

After she slapped a hand over her mouth to hold back a moan, she placed the other one on the top of my head and pushed me closer to her. My mate was learning to take what she wanted and to show me what she needed.

And I wasn't going to hold back tonight.

"Mine," I growled against her pussy, lowering us to the ground.

Once I set her on the dirt, I thrust my fingers into her cunt and continued eating her desperate pussy. She tried to pull her knees together, but I shoved my shoulders between them because I wasn't going to stop.

Tonight, she was all mine. Derrit was gone for now. Our pack-mates were guarding the borders. And my mate had saved all of our lives. This was the least that she deserved. And I would make sure she knew how grateful I was for her.

I pressed my hard cock against the ground and pumped my fingers into her pussy repeatedly, my stubble rubbing on her thighs as I massaged her swollen clit with my tongue. She squirmed in my hold, soft little moans escaping her mouth.

"You're mine," I murmured.

"Yours," she breathed, lacing a hand into my hair and pulling me closer to her.

"Good girl."

She arched her back and moaned, her big tits bouncing. I groaned against her folds, pleasure rushing through my body, and devoured every bit of her. I dropped my tongue even lower to her entrance and licked up her juices as I pounded my fingers into her.

"Beg me to breed you," I growled.

"Please, S-Stone!" she cried, bucking her hips against my mouth. "Put a pup inside me!"

"Louder."

"Please!" she sobbed, hips moving faster.

She was close, but I wasn't going to let her come until I was buried deep inside her and giving her pups. I wanted her to explode around my cock, her pussy gripping tighter and tighter onto it, milking out all my cum.

"P-plea—"

Before she could finish her sentence, I twirled us around so I lay on the dirt and she straddled my waist. Breathing heavily, she dug her fingers into my chest muscle and glided her wet pussy against my pierced cock. And then my mate reached back behind her, took my dick in her hand, and drew her thumb right over the piercing.

Eyes rolling back into my head, I grunted and grasped her wide hips. "I'm going to get you fucking pregnant tonight, mate." And before she could tease me any longer, I slammed myself deep into her cunt.

When she placed her hands on my abdomen to steady herself, I pumped in and out of her like a wild animal. Showing no mercy to that tight pussy. My balls ached every time they slammed against her ass, taunting *me* even more.

The harder I pumped into her, the brighter the whites of her eyes glowed.

And then she suddenly dug her claws into my chest. "*Mark.*"

I slowed my thrusts, cock still buried deep inside her, and stared up at her. "What?"

"Mark," she murmured. "You."

The world around me seemed to slow, and I widened my eyes. "Please," I whispered. I gripped her hips tighter, my fingers curling into her body, and purred.

My wolf fucking purred for her.

"Please," I pleaded again, tilting my head to the side. "Tattoos might cover my entire body, but I've always left this side of my neck bare so I could wear my mate's mark. So, let me wear it. Let me show it off. To you."

A low, possessive growl escaped her lips. Her hands sank around my shoulders as she leaned closer and closer to my chest. When her warm breath fanned my collarbone, I shivered underneath her.

My heart pounded inside my chest, my cock still buried deep inside her. I furrowed my brow and closed my eyes, impatiently waiting for her to claim me like I had wanted her to do since the moment I'd met her.

She moved her mouth up the column of my neck, peppering hungry, sloppy, wet kisses all over me. I pressed her hips against mine, pushing myself as deep as I could get inside her because the moment she marked me … I was going to come.

Deep inside her and give her a pup.

Once she made her way back down my neck to the patch of skin that I hadn't covered in black ink, she paused and gently pricked my skin with the tip of her canines. Another shiver rolled through me.

"Ple—"

Before I could even continue my sentence, sharp canines slid into my flesh. I groaned into her ear, euphoria rushing through my entire body as the mate bond finally solidified between us.

Zuri continued to push her canines into me until her gums pressed against my neck. I lifted my hips, gently teetering them back and forth by a couple of inches as I came inside her pussy. She spasmed on top of me, squeezing my cock with her walls and coming with me.

"Goddess," I breathed, heart pounding. "You're a fucking goddess."

When she growled, the pierced skin vibrated around her teeth. Another wave of pleasure rushed through me, and I dropped my head to the side to give her even better access. My mind was light, floating. And I had never *ever* felt so good.

Once she finally began pulling her teeth from the crook of my neck, she growled the word, "*Mate*," over and over. She licked my mark to seal the wound and to seal our bond underneath the moon gazing down upon us.

"Mate," she murmured, sitting back. Those white eyes slowly faded into her beautiful brown ones as realization crossed her face. And while I expected her to be upset or scared, she smiled down at me. "You're all mine now, Stone. All mine."

CHAPTER
THIRTY-THREE

ZURI

"MORNING, MATE," Stone murmured into my ear the next morning. His heavy arm was slung around my waist, his hand gripping my stomach. He pressed himself against my ass from behind and grazed his teeth against my mark.

"It's too early," I whispered, pushing back against his dick to tease him.

"Too early, huh?"

"Go back to sleep."

He grazed his hand from my belly to my hip, then pulled my asscheeks apart to nestle himself even deeper between them. I arched my back slightly, the heat rushing through my body and not leaving until I slept with him again.

The cursed Moon Goddess had put me into heat all last night —even after I completed the mating process with him—and forced me to fuck this hunk of a man. I didn't know what the hell had possessed her.

But I mean, I wasn't complaining *that* much.

As he kissed the back of my neck, I moaned softly. He ground his cock against my entrance, teasing and taunting me with it.

And all I wanted was for him to push it inside me again and again and again. Like he had all night long.

With his hands roaming up and down my body, he finally pushed me onto my stomach and crawled on top of me from behind in a prone-bone position, his legs on either side of my hips and his cock buried between my thighs.

"Stone," I whined, "I'm so tired."

"You don't have to do a thing," he murmured against my shoulder.

I closed my eyes because the sunlight flooding in through the curtains was so bright this morning as his mouth moved down my spine to my ass and then even lower. He curled his strong arms around my waist and pulled my hips up into the air.

"Stone," I whispered, heat rushing through me.

"I'm so fucking hungry for you," he murmured.

After leaving wet kisses all over my soaked panties, he ripped them off of me with his canines and spit them out on the bed next to me, then dipped his head and pressed his lips to my swollen and aching clit.

I gathered the bedsheets in my fists, tugging on them and moaning softly.

Massaging my clit with his tongue, Stone gripped my thighs tighter. My pussy tightened, and I whimpered as my legs began trembling.

Stone slid a finger into my core and growled ferociously against me, "We're not leaving this bedroom until I come inside my mate again."

"S-S-Stone!" I cried. "You already came inside me five times last night."

"Better chances of getting you pregnant with my pup." He chuckled darkly against me. "Your pussy is clenching at the thought of it. We'd better get you some more of that pregnancy tea, huh? Make sure you drink it every morning before and after I fuck you."

My breath caught, and I arched my back harder for him,

another whimper escaping my throat. "I want you inside of me," I breathed out, tightening even harder the more he shoved his fingers into me. "Please."

With my ass in his huge hands, he crawled back up my body and pressed his pierced cock against my entrance. I pushed back against him, desperate for it. He smacked my ass and slid into me.

I threw my head back as pleasure coursed through my body, and I pulled my thighs together. The Moon Goddess had known exactly what she was doing when she made Stone.

Goddess!

"You're mine," he growled.

"I'm yours," I breathed out, showing him the mark on my neck.

He pounded into me harder and faster, dipping his head to my mark and sucking on it.

"I'm yours!" I cried the harder he sucked.

"Mine," he purred. "All mine."

"Yours. Yours. Yours. Yours. Yours. Yours!" I pleaded like a wolf in heat.

We had already fully completed our mate bond, but the heat felt even hotter than it had the other night. Like I hadn't mated him yet or the Moon Goddess wasn't satisfied with our completion of it.

"More. More. More. More."

"Baby," he murmured against me, "you sound so desperate."

"Please, d-don't pull out!" I cried, pushing my hips back against his. "Please!"

A low growl escaped his lips, and he slammed his cock into me faster and faster. I curled my hands into the sheets and cried out when he stilled deep inside my pussy. My toes curled as the pleasure coursed through my body.

"Curse the Moon Goddess," I whispered, smiling over at him when he collapsed onto the bed beside me, chest rising and falling quickly.

He grinned back at me. "Curse the Moon Goddess for making me mate the sexiest wolf alive. So hot that I have to fuck her every chance I get. SMH."

I playfully shoved his shoulder, then crawled toward him and cuddled into his shoulder. "Shut up."

"You don't mean that, mate," he teased. "Because if you really want me to shut up, you can sit on my face."

Heat surged through me, and I pressed my thighs together, the lingering ache appearing between them yet *again*.

He gently nipped my cheek in his mouth and tugged. "I'll let you rest for now. You wouldn't be able to take another orgasm."

I scoffed. "Yes, I would. *You* wouldn't be able to come inside—"

Before I could finish my sentence, Stone rolled over between my legs and fastened his mouth on my cunt. "Shall we see how many orgasms it takes for you to beg me to stop? Hmm?" he growled, playfulness in his eyes. "Because I can do this all day."

CHAPTER
THIRTY-FOUR

"YOU'RE GLOWING," Sapphire hummed with a big smile on her face.

I had *finally* gotten out of bed with Stone three hours ago, and now, I aided Sapphire with some pack duties. She glanced over my shoulder at Stone, who was helping James with something.

"You both completed the mate bond?! Gah, I'm so happy for you!"

My lips curled into a small smile, and I bit back a giggle. "Last night."

"Finally!" she exclaimed, clapping her hands together. "James and I made a bet that it would happen within a week, especially after last night. We can't wait for you to have pups running around the pack!"

"We need to take care of Derrit before we even think about that," I said.

But secretly, I was super excited to have pups with Stone. While I had completely loathed the man when I first met him, after completing the mate bond with him last night, something had switched inside me.

I wanted to be pregnant by him *yesterday*.

Now, it wasn't a Moon Goddess thing. It was something I wanted. He had made me believe that we could have a functional, nontoxic family together and that I could be a great mother to our kids.

For years, I'd feared that my pups would get bullied like I had.

But if my pups got bullied, Stone would take care of them. Even more than that, Stone would teach our children how to speak up and stand up for themselves, like he had with me. Because he knew what it felt like to be bullied too.

"Oh, come on," she cheered, leaning closer to me. "You can break the rules."

"If I have a baby now, Derrit will hurt it. And I refuse to let him hurt Stone with our pup."

Suddenly, she became quiet. "It could be years."

"What?"

"It could be years before you have a pup then," she whispered, glancing down at the dirt between us and wrapping her arms around her thin body. "We've been fighting Derrit for a long, long time, Zuri."

A frown crossed my lips, and I dropped my gaze too. My stomach twisted and turned, a soft voice drifting through my ear. For a moment, I thought it was Derrit's, but then the Moon Goddess appeared behind Sapphire.

"It won't take that long," the Moon Goddess said. *"You'll be pregnant before the week's end."*

"I'm not putting our pup in danger," I said through my mind to her because I didn't want Sapphire to think I was crazy and talking to myself.

I hadn't discussed my relationship with the Moon Goddess in detail with everyone. It had taken a lot of courage to mention it to the girls yesterday.

"You need to have this pup, Zuri. It's essential," she replied.

"Essential?" I repeated, disbelief and annoyance rushing through my veins. *"How?"*

The Moon Goddess stepped into Sapphire's body, her ghost making Sapphire's skin glow. "You must have this baby," she repeated. "You must have this baby soon. It's the only way you'll defeat Derrit."

"If you know how we're going to defeat him, why can't you just tell me?!" I shouted.

Suddenly, Sapphire's glowing skin disappeared, and she stood in front of me with wide eyes. "Are you okay?" she asked, brow furrowed. She glanced over her shoulder to see empty woods behind us.

My cheeks warmed at my outburst. "Y-yes, I'm fine."

I tightened my hands into fists next to my sides and gritted my teeth. The next time I saw the Moon Goddess, it'd better be while I was alone so I could actually talk to her—or more like scream at her. If she knew how this was all going to end—or more specifically what I needed to do to end this war for good—then why couldn't she tell me?

This was madness!

"Your eyes are glowing again," Sapphire said. "Are you sure you're okay?"

After blinking a handful of times, I watched the brightness fade in Sapphire's pupils. And then I collapsed against a tree, running my hands across my face because I was so freaking tired of not knowing what was going on with me.

"I'm fine, but thank you."

She grabbed my hand. "I should bring you back to Alpha Stone."

"No," I reassured, pulling back. "I'm fine. Really."

While she went to grab my hand again, she stopped inches from my wrist and then pulled her hand away. "Who were you talking to just now?" She glanced over her shoulder again. "Is someone here? Derrit?"

"No," I said, my stomach turning. "It's the Moon Goddess."

Her eyes widened. "The Moon Goddess?! She is here?"

"Was."

"Really?!"

My lips curled into a small smile. "Yes."

"What did she say?"

I swallowed hard and stared at Stone making his way through the forest to us. He must've heard my outburst at Sapphire, which would've never happened if the Moon Goddess had just been honest with me for once.

"Hmm?" Sapphire said.

"She said that I have to get pregnant," I whispered. "For us to win the war."

"How will that help us win the war?" she asked.

"Beats me."

After sniffing the air, Sapphire glanced over her shoulder at Alpha Stone walking toward us with James. Then, she moved closer to me and grasped my hand. "If that's what she said, then you have to do it."

"But … if I get pregnant …"

Derrit would do everything in his power to hurt the baby and me.

"Please, Zuri," Sapphire pleaded. "Derrit almost got my mate killed yesterday. If he keeps this up, then he will eventually wipe this entire pack out. He will hurt our alpha if he forces Alpha Stone or you to kill another one of his packmates. Once you break down the mind …"

"Dark magic is easier to perform on someone."

CHAPTER
THIRTY-FIVE

STONE

"WHAT HAPPENED?" I asked Zuri, grabbing her hand and pulling her back toward the group of warriors that I had been speaking to prior to Zuri's voice booming through the forest at Sapphire.

Zuri's coiled curls blew backward in the slight woodsy breeze as the sunlight made her dark skin glow. She pressed her brown lips together and shuffled beside me, her nerves so intense that I could feel them through the mate bond.

Both Sapphire and Zuri didn't look hurt or angry with each other. Which meant that something else must've happened, but neither of them spoke a word, no matter how many times I asked them about it.

"Nothing," Zuri finally whispered when we approached the warriors.

The midday sun blazed down upon the forest around us. The warriors sat in a circle around a raging fire that we had started hours ago. Maybe it had been burned into our genetics, but we always brainstormed best around an open fire.

Flames flickered, creating grotesque shadows across some warriors' faces. Some were still recovering from the battle yesterday, the light illuminating their bruises and scars. Others had healed completely but were still pissed that Derrit had hurt us this badly.

James tossed a log into the crackling fire. "What's going on?"

Zuri paused in front of us and gazed up at me, a small layer of sweat forming on her forehead from the intense heat. The werewolf warriors all quieted down and gazed at their luna—and the woman who had saved them yesterday—which filled me with pride.

"Something happened, Z," I said. "I'm here to protect you, so tell me."

Zuri ran a hand across her face and blew out a sigh.

Sapphire stepped forward and took Zuri's hand, squeezing it with a smile plastered across her face. "Zuri thought I was the Moon Goddess for a second. She saw her out in the woods."

My eyes widened. "You saw her again? What'd she say?"

"Nothing," Zuri whispered, her voice harsher than usual. After another low breath, she glanced up at me through those pretty brown eyes. "Sorry, but we can't talk about it right here in front of everyone. It's private."

"What is it?" I asked through the mind link.

"A pup."

"A what?" I repeated out loud. "Are you—"

"No," she exclaimed. "Not yet."

"But soon," Sapphire said with a smirk, as if she knew what we were talking about.

"I need to—" Zuri stopped short and glanced over my shoulder and into the woods.

"What's going on?" James asked, peering into the woods. "Derrit?"

"No," Zuri said, releasing Sapphire's hand and walking toward the woods. "It's the Moon Goddess. I need to talk to her."

She paused right next to me and placed a hand on my chest, as if she knew I would put up a fight about her walking through the woods by herself. "Alone."

"Zuri—"

"Stone," she said sternly, "I need to talk to her alone."

After glancing over my shoulder at the empty woods behind me, I balled my hands into tight fists by my sides and growled through my canines, "Don't leave the property. If you need help, yell for me, and I'll be there to save you."

Popping up onto her toes, she kissed me on the lips and smiled. "Thank you."

While she walked toward the empty woods, I fumed in annoyance and hoped that this wasn't another one of Derrit's dirty tricks. He had been using dark magic a bit too much lately, and if he was playing the long game of entering Zuri's mind, then …

We were screwed.

"Have you told her about the prophecy yet?" James asked once she disappeared.

I ran a hand across my face and blew out a deep breath. "Not yet."

"Why not?" another warrior asked.

"It's not a good time. She's too stressed out about everything else right now. This will add to her stress, and if she's not thinking clearly, then it'll be easier for Derrit to slip into her mind and control her."

If that happened, then this entire pack would fall apart. For more than one reason. But the biggest reason being that if I lost her, then I would lose all sense of myself. I would lose the very reason for my existence.

"Have you at least let your grandma talk to her?" Sapphire said. "I'm sure they'd get along quite nicely. And maybe your grandma will be able to see a bit more into the prophecy than she did the first time."

I drew my tongue across the pricks of my canines. Grandma had told me that the Moon Goddess came to her in a dream, but she couldn't make out most of what she had said to her. Or maybe it was that she couldn't quite remember, as it was years and years ago that it had happened.

"I'll talk to her," I said. "Tonight."

CHAPTER
THIRTY-SIX

ZURI

AFTER WALKING AWAY FROM STONE, I followed the aura of the Moon Goddess through the woods. About a quarter mile into the walk, the aura suddenly materialized, and the Moon Goddess stood at a river with another glowing being.

While both women were taller than average and one was about my height, the new woman stood a few inches shorter than us and was a bit more petite with delicate features and a soft smile. Her shoulder-length braids swayed in the breeze against her caramel-colored shoulders.

I slowed down to a cautious walk and glanced between the two. "What's going on?"

The new woman arched her brow at the Moon Goddess. "You didn't tell her?"

"Not yet," the Moon Goddess said. "But it's time we come clean."

Standing elegantly with her fingers intertwined in front of her muted-toned dress, she glanced at the Moon Goddess and shook her head. "I should've known that you would keep it a secret from her for all these years," she said, voice gentle.

And while she had only spoken a few words, I felt drawn to her, like I did with the Moon Goddess, like she had wisdom beyond anyone's years and that if she said anything … I would believe it.

Heart racing, I stepped back and clenched my jaw. "What's going on? Who are you?"

"We're the Moon Goddess," they said in unison.

Confusion coursed through my system, and I gazed at the original goddess that I had been seeing and talking to in my daydreams and regular dreams. "But I thought you were the Moon Goddess," I whispered, unable to make sense of this all.

The other arched a brow at her. "What have you been telling her?"

"What?" The original Moon Goddess giggled. "It's not a lie."

After furrowing my brow, I gazed between them. "What're you talking about?"

"The Moon Goddess isn't one entity, like everyone thinks," the new one said.

"There are three sisters of the moon, sweet child," the original goddess said.

I crossed my arms and glared at her. "I'm not a child."

The only people who were acting like children were the two goddesses—or whatever the hell they were—standing right in front of me and refusing to explain anything or give me the information that I actually needed to fight Derrit.

The ladies looked at each other and giggled behind their hands.

"Baby, you're a child to us," one said.

"We have four thousand years on you."

Gritting my teeth and stopping myself from saying what I really wanted to say to the woman who had lied to me already, I cleared my throat. "If the Moon Goddess is three people, then where is the third?"

"Her spirit drifted away from us twenty-something years ago."

"How?" I asked.

"Long story." The other waved me off. "It will take an eternity to tell you about it."

"So … why are there three sisters of the moon?" I asked, wanting as much information as they would give me.

Because once they left me alone for good, I didn't want to talk to them ever again, especially if they weren't going to give me any decent information.

They kept dancing around with their words.

"One sister to choose mates," the original goddess said. "That's me. Ifa."

"Of course it is," I mumbled under my breath, thinking about when she had forced me through heat so I would mate with Stone and then *watched us* do it. What kind of freak was she?! "I bet you control fertility too, don't you?"

She smirked. "Actually, no."

"I'm the sister of life and death," the other said. "You can call me Shivani."

"And the third?" I asked.

"The third is the protector of wolves, known for her strength and faith," Ifa said.

There was a pause. I expected them to dive deeper into the protector, but they didn't.

"So, do you want to know why people in your old pack didn't like you?" Shivani said.

While I had asked myself that for years, being with Stone made me realize that I didn't quite care anymore. I didn't need to know why they had made fun of me for over two decades or why they had bullied me again and again.

"You know what?" I said defensively. "No, I don't want to know."

Ifa chuckled and threw her arm around my shoulders. "Of course you do."

"No, I—"

Before I could say another word, Shivani looped her arm

around mine and pressed her forefinger to my lips to shush me. "Oh, sweetheart, it doesn't matter if you want to know. You *need* to know now to understand what's gone wrong."

We walked along a path suddenly glowing with moonflowers through the woods. I swore that I had been on this path about a hundred times since moving in with Stone, and I had never seen a moonflower that glowed as brightly as they did now.

"The day you were conceived, your mother's stomach began glowing white," Shivani said, a small smile on her face. "The elders of your old pack thought that your mother and the child she was carrying were cursed by the devil."

"Why is that funny?" I asked, eyeing her smile.

Ifa giggled. "It's funny because we know the true meaning behind it."

Shivani rolled her eyes. "Don't mind her. She's too excited that you're here. We were supposed to wait until you had a child yourself before even talking to you, but as you can see, she couldn't wait."

"Why?" I asked, confused. "Why couldn't you wait to talk to me?"

The sisters gazed at each other, both suddenly silent. A moment passed, then another.

"You can tell her, sister," Shivani said. "Because I know you can't wait."

Ifa moved closer to me and grasped my hands, her lips curling into a smile. "After our sister died, her spirit was transported into the body of an unborn child." She paused for another second. "And that child, Zuri, was you."

My eyes widened. "That means ..."

"That you're a sister of the Moon Goddess. Zuri, the protector."

CHAPTER
THIRTY-SEVEN

ZURI

"A SISTER OF THE MOON GODDESS." The words tumbled out of my mouth, feeling so foreign yet so right.

This explained so much: my *visions*, my power, and my strength that I had found here. But I still had so many unanswered questions.

"How can this be?" I whispered. "Why me? Why now?"

Out of all the wolves that could've been chosen, out of all the wolves who had been conceived the same day that I was, why had I been the one? I hadn't been from any special bloodline and certainly shouldn't have been the first pick.

"Why you?" Shivani asked. "We will never know why our sister's spirit chose your body, but she must've seen the strength inside you to withstand even the harshest blows—emotional, verbal, and physical."

Ifa nodded. "She definitely did."

I glanced between the sisters, who stared at me in complete awe, like I was the most beautiful being that they had ever seen. Like I was something mystical and almost unreal. But I was just Zuri.

"I'm nothing special," I said.

The sisters threw their heads back and giggled with each other, grabbing on to each other's hands for support and wiping tears of laughter from their eyes. When they finally settled down to small chuckles, they smiled at me.

"Oh, child, you have so much to learn about your powers and your history," Ifa said.

"If you could only see the past," Shivani said, "you'd know that you are the most special out of all of us. You've protected the werewolf species from hundreds of enemies, during thousands of battles, from envious gods and goddesses. The wolves wouldn't have survived without you."

Warmth bubbled in my belly, and I … I didn't know how to feel. Had all that really happened? I, or more like my spirit, had saved the werewolf species? And I was here to save them again from Derrit and the monsters who supported him.

"Why now? Why haven't I had this power since birth?" I asked.

"Honestly," the sisters said together, "we don't know."

"But I felt something special inside you materialize once you met Stone," Ifa said.

"So, why do you want me to have pups? Will they help defeat him?"

"Usually, when a she-wolf is pregnant, her body becomes stronger to prepare for the child. Her powers are somewhat … magnified. So, we believe that it will be the same for you. Your powers will become stronger than they are now."

"And"—Ifa giggled—"I can't wait to be an aunt!"

Shivani playfully waved her hand in dismissal. "Don't listen to her."

"Oh, come on," Ifa said, rolling her eyes. "We've sat up talking to the stars about how much we want to have a bigger family that is one of our own, just like our wolves and our creations do."

After leaning against Ifa's shoulder and intertwining their fingers, Shivani smiled softly at me. "We do want to add more to our family. It has only been us three sisters for thousands of years. You're the first one of us who can get pregnant."

"How do you know I can get pregnant?" I asked. "If all of you haven't been able to …"

"Because you're the first one of us to be able to have a mate," Ifa said.

"You naughty rule breaker," Shivani said.

A small laugh left my mouth, my uneasiness subsiding and turning into … something light, something easy, something comfortable. And the feeling of having been with them forever seemed to make me happy.

For so long, I had been without anyone who truly cared for me. It was so refreshing to know that I would have Ifa and Shivani for years and years and years to come. No matter what. They were my family, and they'd been alone too.

"How did your past sister … die?" I whispered.

The girls looked at each other and frowned.

"Ifa and I have been here since the beginning of time, along with many of the other gods and goddesses. We usually live forever, but after millennia of taking the brunt of the pain away from the wolves, all the hurt and torture they bore, our sister took from them so they wouldn't hurt anymore. She had been sick for a while."

Ifa cleared her throat. "And then a child of dark magic was born."

"Derrit," I whispered.

"Yes, and she vowed to rid the world of him. She told us that she had visions of destruction if he lived."

"We begged her not to go." Ifa sniffled, a tear running down her cheek.

"She wasn't strong enough."

"But she was too stubborn, and she left in the early morning while we slept."

"She left," Shivani whispered, hanging her head, "and never came back."

The girls paused for a moment until Ifa tightened her hold on Shivani's hand and stepped forward. "We later found out that she had traveled to kill the baby in order to protect wolves for generations to come. She should've waited for us to aid her, but Shivani knew that her power of death couldn't stop magic that dark."

"It's said that as soon as our sister touched the baby, she crumbled to pieces."

"I'm sorry about your sister, but ..." I started. Nerves bubbled in my stomach, twisting at my insides as the worries played through my mind on repeat. "What if that happens to me too? What if we can't kill him?"

"You can," the sisters said in unison.

"You have the power of protection inside you, and once you start training regularly, your body will remember everything that happened to her in the past. Your body will remember the battles she fought, the weapons she used, and the protection that she did."

"Besides, our sister was much weaker from years of tear on her body."

While I seemed to be the only chance for the wolves, especially if the last sister had died, I had to fight. But all I could seem to think about was Stone.

Would I not age while he did? Would I have to see my mate die one day? And what about our pups? Would they be immortal too?

"You still have questions," Shivani noted. "Please ask."

"I'm not sure if I want to know the answers."

"If you don't ask now, you will surely learn the answers later."

I gulped down my fear. "What will happen to Stone?"

"Stone?" Shivani said. "You mean ..."

"In eighty years, when I'm supposed to be on my deathbed, what will happen to him?"

Shivani paused, then looked at Ifa. "Can you do anything for her?"

Ifa paused and dropped her gaze to the ground. "I can't make mates immortal."

"That means … he'll die?"

They answered me in silence.

Tears welled up in my eyes. I needed to find Stone.

THIRTY-EIGHT

STONE

"KNOCK, KNOCK," I said, peering into Grandma Bee's house through the screen door.

"Stoney," she said, voice hoarse and slow. "Is that you?"

I watched her stand from the couch and hobble over, her back hunched. "Yes, it's me."

Once she unlocked the door and let me inside her house, Grandma slowly walked to the fridge and pulled it open with a shaky hand. After taking out two beers, she strolled back to the table covered with a plaid plastic tablecloth and fumbled with the tab.

"I'll do that for you, Grandma," I said, taking them from her and opening both.

Once she took a long gulp, she exhaled in relief. "Where's Zuri? You need to bring her around more," she said, waggling her finger at me. "I know how you alphas are, wanting to get your mates pregnant as quickly as possible. But you need to let that girl breathe."

"She's"—I paused—"talking to the Moon Goddess."

"What?!" she exclaimed. "The Moon Goddess?"

"Yes. I've actually come to talk about the prophecy."

Grandma Bee stiffened. "What prophecy?"

I arched my brow. "Grandma, you know what prophecy I'm talking about."

"In my old age," she said, gulping down more beer, "I don't remember anything."

But she wasn't looking at me anymore, and that light expression had dropped from her face, replaced with guilt. She knew exactly what I was talking about, but for some reason, she didn't want to talk about it.

"The prophecy that came to you a couple of years ago," I clarified. "About this pack."

She finished the beer in two more gulps, then headed to the fridge for a second. "Stoney, that prophecy was more like a dream to me. I barely remember it. It might not even be true." She opened the fridge and stared into it. "Moon Goddess, I hope it's not."

"Why not?"

"Because … that'd mean that Zuri isn't your mate. And—"

"What do you mean?" I asked because this was the first time I was hearing this.

"The prophecy mentioned a goddess," she finally said. "Not a werewolf who can wield magic. The alpha of this pack is supposed to be mated with someone who is much, much stronger than Zuri." Another pause. "But Zuri makes you so happy. And I haven't seen you this much at peace in decades."

"You didn't tell me this," I whispered, my stomach turning.

While I wanted to believe in this prophecy because it would help us defeat Derrit, I couldn't even fathom the thought of being with someone other than Zuri. She was my everything. The woman I would do anything for.

Even if it meant saving my pack, I would never reject her. Never give her up.

I refused to ever even think of another wolf the way that I thought about Zuri. She was mine forever, and we would have to find another way. Even if I lost everyone else … I would sacrifice the world in order to live and die with her as my mate.

"I wasn't sure what I saw at the time," she said. "But Zuri is an amazing girl, and I didn't want to tell you because I didn't want to hurt you, Stoney. You love her."

My hands balled into fists, and I shoved my chair back, the legs screeching against the wooden floorboards. Why hadn't she told me about this? Why hadn't she fucking told me? All this time … all this fucking time …

"Stoney, where are you going?" Grandma Bee asked.

"For a run."

And with that, I pushed through the door and headed into the woods to clear my head. I shifted into my wolf, clothes tearing, and propelled myself through the forest to find Zuri. I needed to be with her right now.

I wouldn't tell her about the prophecy. No fucking way. I didn't want her to worry that I would leave her for someone else just so we could defeat Derrit. Fuck the prophecy. We would do it together.

When I spotted her rushing through the woods toward the pack house, I ran over to her and shifted into my human form in front of her. She widened her beautiful brown eyes and ran over to me, placing her head on my chest.

"Stone," she breathed out, her fingers curling against my chest.

"I've been looking for you," I hummed. "We need to talk."

She gently shook her head. "I need to tell you something first."

"What is it?" I asked, but when she dropped her head and a wave of fear rushed through our link, I scooped up her face into my hands and forced her to look at me. "What's going on, Zuri? What did the Moon Goddess say?"

"She wasn't the Moon Goddess," Zuri whispered.

"What?" I growled, canines lengthening. My entire body stiffened, and a hundred thousand ways that I could kill that fucker

Derrit played through my mind. "If he fucking hurt you, Zuri, then I'm going to—"

She glanced up at me and furrowed her brow. "What're you talking about?"

"Derrit."

"That woman wasn't Derrit either," she said.

Anger slowly subsiding, I shook my head. What was she saying? If she wasn't the Moon Goddess or Derrit, then who had she been talking to? Had she been lying to me? Was it even a woman? Maybe … I bit back another growl. No, she wouldn't do that.

Zuri and I were mated. We both fucking felt the bond.

But as the moments passed without her saying anything, all I could think was the worst.

"Why don't you want to tell me?" I whispered.

"It's not that I don't want to tell you," she said, lips quivering. "I'm scared."

"About?"

After drawing her fingers up my tattooed arms, she set them on my shoulders and lifted her gaze to meet mine once more. Tears welled in her now-glowing golden eyes, threatening to spill over and down her cheeks. "I don't want anything to happen to us."

"Nothing will."

"You can't tell anyone," she whispered.

"You think I'd tell anyone?"

"The Moon Goddess isn't one entity, like you think she is, but instead, she is three sisters who rule by each other's sides. One sister for mates. One sister for life and death. One for protection. I've been talking to Ifa, the sister of mates, who has bound me to you."

"Three sisters?" I repeated, confused as hell.

There was no way that the Moon Goddess could be three sisters. We—my pack and every other pack—had prayed to a singular Moon Goddess since the beginning of time. Never had I heard of there being three sisters, even in myths.

"I know. I know …" she said. "I didn't believe it either at first, but it's true."

"What about the other sisters? Have you met them?"

She paused. "Yes, the sister of life and death is named Shivani. I met her today."

"And the third? Was she there?" I asked because we could really use her to protect all of us from the devil that was Derrit, my asshole brother who I had vowed to murder one day. I would do anything, strike any deal, to have her on our side.

"Yes," my mate whispered.

"And?"

"And her name is Zuri."

STONE

"WHAT?" I whispered, heart racing. "The third goddess is you?"

My mate stood in front of me, clutching my biceps and smiling softly up at me. "I guess so, but I mean … I'm not sure. How can I be a goddess? How can I wield that much power? And to protect everyone against Derrit?"

Eyes widening slightly, I stared down at her and shook my head, unable to wrap my head around it. My mate *was* a goddess, unlike what Grandma Bee had said. My mate wasn't just a wolf who could wield magic. She was a fucking goddess!

"And they mentioned that if I get pregnant—"

"If?" I growled, tossing her over my shoulder with ease and heading through the forest to the pack house. "*If* is not part of this conversation. *When* you get pregnant, Zuri. Because I'm not letting you leave our bed without a pup in your belly."

"Hey!" Zuri exclaimed suddenly. "Get out of here! You're not going to watch."

A chuckle escaped my throat as I glanced around the forest. "Are they here?"

Because I wanted to thank whichever goddess it was for mating me with Zuri. We all knew that I didn't deserve someone as strong as her, someone as sweet, as good, as godly as her. But I wasn't going to let my chances go.

She was mine. She was a goddess. And she needed my pup.

"They're gone now," Zuri said, her body feeling plumper and ready to bear children.

Once I slipped into the pack house with Zuri, I headed straight for the bedroom.

"If they are right and you have more power than you know, then if you really didn't want this, you could've slithered out of my hold and kicked me in the balls so hard that I could *never* give you pups."

She stiffened in my arms and pressed her thighs together. "Stone."

I tossed her onto the bed and watched as she landed on the pillows. Zuri leaned back against the headboard, nipples taut ... and her mark glow against the orange sunlight.

"If you don't want me to give you a pup right now, your tight little cunt wouldn't be drooling through your shorts for me," I murmured, dropping my gaze to her thighs pressed together, the scent of her arousal drifting off her in waves.

She sucked in a breath.

"Spread your legs, *mate*," I said.

Eyes glinting gold, she furrowed her brow and whimpered. And then, just as I had asked—*demanded*—she inched her thighs apart until I had enough room to crawl up between them and enjoy every bit of her.

"What are you going to do to me?" she said in a breathy whisper, leaning back on her hands. Her nipples were pressed against her shirt, teasing and taunting me to suck on them. Without mercy. Until she was crying in my hold.

I crawled onto the bed slowly, like a predator eyeing his prey and readying to pounce. She sucked in another sharp breath, her pussy tightening before I could even touch her, and then she dropped her legs to the sides to give me even better access.

"Good girl," I praised, lowering myself onto my stomach. I laid one of her thighs over my left shoulder and gripped the other in my opposite hand to keep her legs spread, no matter how much she wanted to pull them together as I went down on her. Then, I ripped off her shorts.

"Stone," she murmured, eyes blazing now. She cupped my chin and forced me to look up into those beautiful eyes that belonged to *my* goddess. "I asked you a question. And I expect an answer." Her lips curled into a smile. "As your mate."

"As my mate or as my goddess?" I asked, lips brushing against her clit as I talked. I gazed at her through my brows, lowering my mouth another millimeter. "If you wanna play the role of domme tonight, then play it well, Zuri. Tell me what I'm going to do to you. Don't ask."

Another wave of arousal rushed through her, her pussy beginning to dribble onto the bed.

"Come on," I taunted her, lowering my lips another millimeter. "What am I going to do?"

"Y-you're going to," she said, cheeks flushing in embarrassment, "eat my pussy."

My lips curled into a smile. "Am I?"

"Yes." After straightening her back, she released my chin and instead fisted my dark hair and pulled my face down against her wet cunt. "You're going to eat my pussy, *mate*. And then you're going to put a pup inside me."

After dipping my head, I sucked her clit between my lips and flicked my tongue back and forth across it. She threw her head against the pillows and arched her back, crying out in pleasure as I devoured her pussy.

"More," she moaned. "Please, Stone!"

"Don't ask, Zuri," I murmured, plunging a finger into her. "Demand."

"More!" she cried, demanded. "Push another finger inside me."

I thrust a second and third finger into her tight pussy, stretching her out to prepare her for pushing myself into her and giving my goddess everything that she desired later. Her legs trembled around me, but I continued to eat that cunt like it was my last meal, my tongue massaging that sensitive little bud.

"Oh my Goddess," she murmured, lacing both her hands into my hair and tugging down on my head so I couldn't move. Suddenly, her body stiffened harder than it ever had, her breath caught in her throat.

She was still for a moment. And then she exploded around my fingers.

Doubling down, I buried my face into her cunt and continued to eat her until she finished riding out her orgasm for minutes. When she finally released her grip on my hair, I licked my lips and crawled up between her legs.

"What do you want?" I growled, trailing my fingers up the center of her body to her throat. I wrapped my hand around her neck and gently choked her until she smiled up at me. "*What* do you want?"

"Put a pup inside me, Stone."

Before she could say another word, I slammed into her tight hole and grunted when her pussy wrapped around me like it had been made for my cock. Her moans gave me nothing but satisfaction. I would do anything to hear them every day for the rest of my life.

"Beg for it," I growled, shoving myself into her.

She threw her head against the pillow, legs trembling.

"Beg, Zuri. I want to hear you—"

"A goddess doesn't beg," she said, eyes glowing. Although I could tell that she wasn't totally confident in the words that had escaped her mouth, I wasn't going to let her know that I saw right through her feigned confidence. I wanted to make her strong. Powerful.

"Then, tell me to beg," I murmured.

She tightened around me and sucked in a surprised breath. "I … Stone … I …" She paused for a moment, then turned her lips up into a small smile. "Beg to come inside me, *mate*. Beg for it, Stone."

A low grunt escaped my mouth, dick twitching inside her. "Please, let me come inside you, baby." I dipped my head and rested my forehead against hers. "Let me come inside you and please you. I want to give you pups so badly. Please, Zuri …"

And as the words left my mouth, she exploded around me and grabbed on to my shoulders. "Come with me." Her eyes rolled back into her head. "Come with me, Stone. Give me all of you."

ZURI

THE NEXT MORNING, my head rose and fell on Stone's muscular chest. I fluttered my eyes open and squinted toward the window, where the sunlight flooded into the room, everything suddenly so … quiet.

"How'd you sleep?" Stone mumbled.

I glanced up to see his eyes still closed but a small smile on his face.

"Good, but we should get up to begin training for the day. Sina, Maxine, and Olenna plan to come over today. And I suspect two goddesses will show up to train me too." I glanced over my shoulder, expecting them to be looming over me.

But the room was empty.

Did that mean that we hadn't conceived a pup last night? I was sure they'd be all over me if I had. But on the other hand, usually, they were bothering me that I wasn't trying hard enough to have a pup right here and right now.

A knock sounded at the door. I picked my head up from Stone's chest and sniffed the air, smelling Sina and Maxine in the hallway.

After covering myself, I hopped out of bed and opened the door a couple of inches. "Yes?"

"Olenna is down at the training field," Sina said. "Are you ready to train?"

"I'll be down in a couple of minutes," I said with a smile.

Once I closed the door, Stone tore the blanket I had covering my body away and tossed it onto the bed. He drew his arms around my stomach from behind and pulled me closer so his nose was buried into the crook of my neck.

"Train hard for me today, *mate*, and maybe I'll beg to come inside you again tonight."

Heat coursed through my body, and I twirled in his hold. "Is that right?"

"If you *make* me beg for it," he hummed, pressing his hard cock against my stomach. He tucked some coily hair behind my ear and smirked. "Can my little mate, *my goddess*, do that for me? Hmm?"

"Maybe ..." I giggled.

He chuckled and smacked my ass. "You'd better get out there before I toss you back onto that bed and fuck you until you can't move." He grabbed his shirt from the bed and pulled it onto my body. "My scent is all over you, sweetheart, as a reminder that no matter how hard you train, you still wear my mark. You're still my mate to protect."

My lips curled into a small smile. I stood on my toes to kiss his lips, then ran out of the room before he kept his word on his promise. Or ... before I decided to take him up on it. Because I didn't trust myself after last night.

Once I made it out of the pack house and to the training field, the girls were ... talking to the sister goddesses as if they could see them clearly now. I furrowed my brow and slowed down to a stop.

"You can see them?" I asked the girls.

Stone and the other warriors from his pack couldn't see the other goddesses, but I had always been able to. What did it mean if Sina, Maxine, and Olenna could see them too? Did they all have powers, some that they weren't aware of?

"We come to wolves in dreams, but to those who are worthy in the daytime," Ifa said.

"Worthy?" I asked. "How do you know? How do you *choose* if someone is worthy?"

Shivani's lips curled in a small smile, and she glanced at her sister. "Those who are worthy are the ones who hold immense power within themselves, whether physical, emotional, or mental. And …"

"Only females." Ifa snickered.

"Only females?" I repeated, still confused.

"Because, dear sister," Ifa said, curling her arm around mine and walking toward the training field, "*you* might enjoy all the testosterone from all the alpha males and their warriors around you, but we don't."

Shivani waved her hand dismissively. "It gets old after a few thousand years."

"More like a few *hundred* years," Ifa said.

Shivani rolled her eyes. "If you haven't picked up on it yet, Ifa loves to exaggerate."

Well, while Stone had had *a lot* of testosterone last night, he had made me the one in charge. He had let me boss him around, domme him. My cheeks flushed. I was sure that I had done it all wrong, but he'd seemed to love it.

An alpha male like *him*, begging for me?!

Goddess, I couldn't wait for it to happen again and again and again tonight.

"Did you train last night?" Sina asked, eyes dropping to my thigh. "You look bruised."

"Oh"—Ifa giggled—"she *trained* all right."

I narrowed my eyes. "Ifa!"

"What?!" she exclaimed. "We keep tabs on you. You're our sister and still a little baby in our eyes. We gotta make sure that you're being treated right." She wiggled her eyebrows. "And, you know, that you'll give us a pup."

"Don't worry," Shivani said. "We didn't watch."

I paused for a moment. "Did we …"

When I didn't continue my sentence, the sisters looked at each other in confusion. My cheeks reddened because I *did not* want to say this out loud, and I played with my fingers, gesturing obviously to my stomach.

"I think she's trying to ask if there is a pup in her belly," Ifa said to Shivani.

Shivani shrugged. "Not something I can tell you."

"You're literally the goddess of pups," I reasoned.

She smiled and brushed some hair out of my forehead. "You get to live your life with your mate. You get to discover if you have or don't have a pup on your own, like all she-wolves do. Because this will be the only life that you get with him, and you deserve to live it normally and to be happy with him."

FORTY-ONE

STONE

AFTER ZURI LEFT our bed this morning to train, I walked down to the training area and leaned against a wooden post-and-rail fence and watched her laugh with Sina, Maxine, Olenna, and what I assumed were the other two goddesses that I couldn't see.

Grandma Bee hobbled up next to me.

"You were wrong," I murmured, not to rub it into her face, but because I was happy that she had been wrong about Zuri. Zuri was the goddess of her dreams, my mate, and most importantly, the woman who would save all of us.

"Wrong about what, Stone?"

I side-eyed her and arched my brow. "No Stoney today, Grandma?"

She intertwined her fingers in front of her body and rocked back and forth on her feet, like she usually did. "Sorry, Stoney. I'm not feeling too well today. I think I ate something bad last night after you left."

"What'd you eat?"

"Some berries that I'd gathered from the forest," she said, her hand on her stomach.

"The ones in your fridge? Where'd you get them?" I asked, crossing my arms and giving her my full attention. We had cleared out all the poisonous fruit from the forest a couple of years ago. "There shouldn't be any poisonous berries within our property."

"It could be my stomach," she said. "It's not the same as it was years ago."

Gaze flickering back to Zuri, I nodded. "Let me know if it gets worse, okay?"

"Will do," she said, patting my shoulder. "Now, what was I wrong about?"

"Zuri," I said with a smile, watching as she moved with ease, her brown skin glimmering underneath the sunlight. She was tall, strong, and so fucking perfect. And knowing that she was a goddess … made her even more beautiful. "She's a goddess."

"A goddess?" Grandma Bee repeated in a whisper, fear written all across her face. She glanced up at me through wide, almost-glowing eyes and shook her head. "What do you mean? Like the Moon Goddess?"

I paused. "Are you sure you're okay, Grandma? You look like you're about to—"

Suddenly, fury replaced the fear on Grandma's face, and she lunged at me. Before I could react, her talons ripped through the flesh on my chest, right down to the bone. Blood seeped out of my wound.

"What are you doing?"

"What I should've done a long time ago!" she growled, shifting into her silver wolf.

Last time I had seen it, she could barely shift. And her wolf had looked so weak. But today, she looked reborn. Her wolf might've been silver, but her body was stronger than anything I had seen from her in a while.

Shuffling back, I shook my head. "Grandma, you're sick."

"I'm not sick, *Stoney*," she said, stalking toward me. "Zuri is making *you* sick."

My nails lengthened into claws, my canines extending past my lips. I didn't want to hurt her, but if she lunged at me again, then I would put her in her place. As much as I'd vowed to never touch her, she was speaking nonsense.

"You know what I think?" I said, chest tight. "I think you've been corrupted by Derrit."

As soon as his name left my lips, she leaped into the air and lunged straight at my chest, right for my fucking heart. Tears filled my eyes at the thought of having to hurt my own grandmother, who had been through everything with me.

Just before she could jump down onto me and cut me open with those talons, I grabbed her by the throat and hurled her halfway across the forest. When she hit a tree, it snapped in half and fell close to the training field, her attention shifting from me to Zuri, who yelped.

"Don't fucking think about it," I growled through the mind link to Grandma Bee.

Without a second thought, she sprinted toward my mate at full speed, faster than I had ever seen her run before. I leaped into the air and shifted into my wolf, running twice as fast to cut her off before she had the chance to hurt my mate.

Thick saliva dripped from her extended canines. I pushed myself even harder as she approached Zuri and pushed her out of the way before she could even see me. Grandma latched her canines into my thigh and ripped a chunk of flesh right from me.

Pain split through my body, but I jumped up as soon as Grandma Bee did. She turned on Zuri once more, snarling through her bloody canines and spitting my flesh at her. When Grandma's feet left the ground, I lunged at her body and snapped my teeth around her ankle. Her bone popped underneath my grasp, and another pain—this time emotional—rushed through me.

Grandma was still in there somewhere, her body was still so fragile, but she was corrupted. And I didn't know if I could bring her back around without killing her.

"Stone!" Zuri shouted, brushing herself off. "What's going on?"

While she had the power to protect us, this was my grandmother. I had to do this myself—my chest tightened even more, blood pouring out of it from the wound that she had left in it—even if it meant killing her.

"Stay away from her," I said to Zuri through the mind link. *"She's dangerous. Corrupted."*

With Grandma Bee's leg still in my mouth, I whipped her through the air and smashed her body into the dirt. More bones cracked from the impact, and I pushed back the tears. If her bones broke, then maybe Derrit would leave her. Maybe she wouldn't be of use to him anymore because he couldn't fight with her.

But something told me that wouldn't happen.

Derrit wanted me to kill Grandma Bee to weaken my fucking mind.

And it was working. Goddess, it was fucking working.

After her opposite knee snapped, I released her from my grasp. But somehow, someway, she hopped right back up on broken bones and continued running at my mate, her legs wobbling and moving in ways that they shouldn't. I cursed at the devil who had done this to her and lunged at her, seizing her throat in my canines this time.

Before she could make it to Zuri a second time, I bit down and snapped her neck. She continued to seize in my hold, attempting to break free and escape so she could hurt my mate, but I ripped out her throat and then her heart.

Then, I dropped her twitching body from my mouth and shifted into my human. I lay over Grandma and drew her body into my arms, holding back the tears because I had been the one to cause this and to kill her.

She had been with me since the beginning, had left Derrit and my father's cruel rule, and now … I had killed her because of them. I had given up one of the closest people to me in order to protect my pack and my mate.

Did that make me a monster? Well, I didn't care.

Because I would do it again in a heartbeat.

CHAPTER
FORTY-TWO

ZURI

"ARE YOU OKAY?" I asked Stone, crouching down behind him as he held his grandma.

"Derrit corrupted her," Stone said. "He wanted me to kill her to hurt me."

My body stiffened, and I scanned the forest for any sight of Derrit *or* anyone who might be suspicious. How'd Derrit get in to see Grandma Bee? I didn't know her that much, but she seemed very strong from what Stone had told me.

"We shouldn't be out in the open," I said, stomach twisting. "Let's go to the pack house."

I wanted to make sure that Stone was okay, especially mentally, before storming off to war against Derrit for forcing him to do this. But Stone was an alpha, and alphas didn't like to seem weak, so I was prepared to fight him in order to bring him home.

To ensure his sanity.

"I need to bury her first," Stone said, picking her up.

"We shouldn't right now," I said. "Derrit is probably watching and waiting to get you alone, so he can do the same sick thing to you. Why don't you let the pack doctors look at her to see if we can figure out a cure or a vaccine to stop this from happening in the future?"

"Zuri," Stone growled, "she's my grandma."

"And I'm your mate," I reasoned, lowering my voice. "I know he will break you if he finds you alone right now." I placed my hand on top of his and stared up at him through soft eyes. "Please, let them look at her. Then, you can bury her the way you want. Okay?"

Though his canines were bared, as if he didn't really want to release her, he let her go when Sina took her from his arms. She glanced at me, as if she knew what to do, and walked with Maxine to the pack doctor.

When they were gone, I glanced over at Olenna and the goddesses. They disappeared through the forest, too, leaving me alone with my mate and the deafening silence that followed.

Stone stared emptily at the woods surrounding us. "I'm going to kill him."

"We're going to kill him," I said. "You're not alone."

After a couple of moments of silence, Stone shifted his gaze to me. "You've gotten so strong. So much stronger than I could ever be, Zuri." Heavy tears welled in his eyes, but he pushed them back. "I love you."

"I love you, too, and I want to protect you," I murmured, thinking about what the other goddess—my sisters, as they'd called themselves—had told me not once, but twice now. That he wouldn't be with me forever. "I want to protect you from everything."

Increase his life span as much as I could.

I had only known him for a little bit, but I couldn't imagine my life without him in it. He had made me so strong, and he had made me *believe* that I could do anything I wanted. And believing was the hardest part.

"Why are you saying it like that?" Stone asked.

"Like what?"

"Like there's more that you're not telling me."

Fuck.

I blew out a low breath and shook my head. "I didn't want to tell you because I don't want you to worry or … honestly, even think the way that I am. But the other goddesses told me that … that we won't … be together forever."

He pushed some hair out of my face. "Fuck that, Zuri. We're going to be mates forever, and nobody is going to change that. And if they try to, then I'll kill them for it. Because you've been mine since the moment I laid my eyes upon you."

After laying my hands on his chest, I frowned and whispered the words that I'd wished I never had to, the ones that broke me down so deep to the fucking bones, "Nobody, but death, will take me away from you."

While I expected him to freak out like I was on the inside, he smirked at me. "Little mate, not even death is going to take me away from you. I might not live as long as you do. I might not get to spend every last moment of your life with you. But I can give you a pup who will always have a part of me." He leaned his forehead against mine and sucked my bottom lip between his teeth. "You're never going to be alone in this world."

Still, I refused to let that happen. I vowed to find a way to make him live forever. I vowed to find a way to make him immortal with me. To become as strong as a god in order for him to be with me every waking moment of my life.

"Listen to me," I said, grabbing his chin. "I'm going to do whatever I can—"

Suddenly, the world around me became quiet, and I couldn't even hear myself talk anymore. I pressed my lips together and scanned the forest around me, nerves bubbling up in the pit of my stomach.

"*Zuri,*" Stone said through the mind link, voice so quiet, "*what's going on?*"

I furrowed my brow and listened to branches snapping what must've been miles from here, birds flapping their wings quickly, as if to fly away from something, someone … or maybe a group of people.

"They're coming," I whispered.

Howls echoed through the forest, but when I turned back toward Stone, he didn't seem like he had heard them. Cries for help from women, children, and men drifted through my ears from the south. I craned my head in the direction and pointed.

"They're coming," I said again, this time sure of it. I released Stone's chin from my hand and followed the sounds of war and of battle, my body moving on its own. I couldn't stop myself or think this through.

All my body, my wolf, and my mind wanted was to end this war right here and right now. It was as if this feeling was in my blood, this response in my veins. As if the power from the goddess before me was suddenly seeping through every crevice of me.

"Gather the pack," I said to Stone. "We're ending this now."

CHAPTER
FORTY-THREE

ZURI

"YOU SHOULD STAY HERE." Stone walked beside me to the warrior wolves standing at the edge of our property. "I need to protect you, and if you go to battle, then … I would never forgive myself if something terrible happened to you."

I had never once been in a battle of this caliber. My strength as a Moon Goddess against that of a wielder of dark magic? Who knew the outcome? The other magic wielders had shown me that even as a goddess, I wasn't immortal. But still, I wasn't backing down now.

After taking his chin in my hand, I stared up at him. "You're not going anywhere without me. You've said it yourself that I am strong, so you'd better truly believe it. We will fight together, and we will defeat him."

Honestly, I wasn't sure where all this confidence was coming from—most of it was fake and so foreign to me—but I needed to be strong for this pack. If I showed weakness to them, then they'd lose faith in the Moon Goddess and in me.

"The wolves are prepared to run," James said to us. "We're ready whenever you are."

While I expected Stone to glare down at me in anger because I wasn't listening to his orders, he curled his lips into a small smile, seized my hips, and drew me toward him. "Goddess, I fucking love you."

He sucked my bottom lip between his teeth and tugged on it, and pleasure rolled through my body. He groped me in his strong hands, then suddenly tensed as his fingers brushed against my stomach.

"What is it?" I asked.

"Nothing," he said quickly. "It's nothing at all."

Though there was something.

"Stone, what is it?"

"There is a power inside you." He rested his forehead against mine, his mind racing but so quickly that I couldn't decipher any of the thoughts. "One that I don't recognize yet, but one that is making you stronger."

I tensed and stared up at him. "A power?"

When I had talked to the other Moon Goddesses, they had told me that getting pregnant and having a pup could make me stronger, that it could enhance some of my powers. If that was the case and I was really pregnant with Stone's pup …

"We have to go now," I said, refusing to think about it and refusing to give *him* any time to think about it either. If I did, he might force me to stay home. No way was that happening. Not when Stone was so vulnerable after killing his grandmother unwillingly.

Derrit would suffer for that. I would make sure of it.

I seized Stone's hand. "We're going."

"To kill this fucker for good." He intertwined his fingers with mine and nodded. "James! Contact Carve, Sina, and Xorgor. If Derrit wants to play with dark magic, then we will have the strongest in the kingdom against him. A warlock, a Paragon, and the king of demons."

"I'm going to show you my strength," I whispered to Stone while we marched through the forest toward the sounds of battle.

The scent of blood seeped into my nose. With that much blood, Derrit must've killed hundreds of wolves already just outside of Durnbone. If Olenna, Sina, and Maxine didn't know about them yet, they would surely find out soon enough.

"You already have, *mate*," Stone said, his canines lengthening at the sounds of howls.

An unfamiliar power swelled inside me. "I'm just getting started."

James, who had been a bit behind us, cleared his throat. "This time, we all come back alive. I refuse to bury another packmate."

"We'll all come out of this battle alive, James. We're all stronger than we've ever been." Stone squeezed my hand and glanced down at me, as if his words had a double meaning.

Had the other goddesses told him that I was stronger while pregnant? Did he know?

The closer we approached the battle, the faster we ran. I didn't want to wait any longer, and hearing the cries of wolves falling hurt my soul. I was supposed to protect them, but I wasn't sure if I could protect *anyone*. I still didn't know how to use my powers. We hadn't gotten that far in training yet.

But as we passed the last line of trees and stepped into the clearing, I stopped. Bodies of wolves littered the battlefield, so many that I could barely move forward without stepping on the corpse of a warrior wolf. The stench of blood burned my nose.

Slowly, I moved through the wolves, my lips quivering at just how many had died, just how many I hadn't been able to protect. Stone pulled me forward, toward the battle that had moved deeper into the clearing.

"Derrit is up ahead," Stone said through his canines. "I smell his stench."

Our packmates had already shifted into their wolves and joined the fight, but Stone had stayed with me the entire time, walking through the field as my body seemingly collected the last of the energy from the corpses.

These wolves had stood no chance.

Energy swelled inside me. We walked further onto the battle-field, this time ready to fight. I wanted Derrit's blood on the ground, like he had done to so many of my wolves. Yet canines gleamed as the wolves howled their last breaths. Blood was splat-tered everywhere on the battlefield. I scanned the forest.

"Where the fuck is he?" I growled, my eyes darting from one direction to the next.

Derrit had always been a coward, never one to take on a fight head-on and always having to use other people's bodies to do his dirty work.

He preferred to slink in the shadows, waiting for the perfect moment to strike. Take the form of friendly wolves in order to buy himself time and get closer to us. But not now. No. I fucking refused. He had crossed a line, and he would pay for it.

The trees rustled to my left, catching my attention. A lone wolf emerged from them, his fur matted with blood and his eyes narrowed in fury.

Derrit bared his teeth and shifted into his human form, spit-ting a wad of flesh toward us. "*Stoney*, Zuri ... you've finally arrived. I've been waiting for you."

FORTY-FOUR

ZURI

WITH HIS PACK gathered around him, baring their canines at us, Derrit stood across the forest and smirked at me. His eyes glimmered with a magic so dark, as if he had been waiting and preparing for this fight since the last time I had seen *him*, not in someone else's body.

His black tattoos lifted off his body, and mists of blackness swirled around him. My heart raced in my chest, and I swallowed hard.

Had those tattoos been dark magic all along? Did he bring it everywhere that he went?

Screw it, I don't have time to think.

I balled my hands into tight fists. My pack rested on my shoulders. And while I might've been part Moon Goddess now, who was supposed to be the protector of wolves, I didn't know the first thing about fighting a man who wielded dark magic.

But I had to fight him if I wanted to save my pack.

"You think you can defeat me, Zuri?" he taunted, his eyes gleaming with malice. "Don't let my brother fool you into thinking that you're anything more than a rogue, a rut"—he chuckled—"a whore who would do anything to be accepted."

A ferocious growl escaped my mate's lips as he stepped forward, but I stayed by his side the entire time. Stone was still hurting from killing his grandma. I could feel his pain through our mate bond, so I couldn't let Derrit corrupt him.

"Don't feed his hatred," I said to my mate through the mind link.

Sparks of power ignited my fingertips. I glanced down at them to see white light traveling up the length of my brown digits and then forming a ring of power in the center of my palms, the energy more powerful than I had ever felt before.

"If you turn her over to me, I vow not to attack you for the rest of eternity," Derrit offered.

For a moment, my thoughts wavered at what the pack would choose for me. It was a decent offer, one that I wasn't sure that Derrit could uphold, but nonetheless, if it was true, then they would all be saved.

"Fuck you," Stone growled.

"We're not handing anyone over to you," James said.

The rest of the wolves in our pack followed suit and growled at Derrit. And I had never once felt more power, more happiness and joy, more protected than I had in that moment. They all were willing to risk their lives to save me, and I had to do the same for them.

Derrit growled, his eyes turning from a brown to a blazing black. The dark magic around him intensified, the air thick and heavy with impenetrable mist. We had to act quickly before he could launch an attack.

We had to be the predator. Not the prey.

So, I closed my eyes and focused on the power within me, drawing it out through my palms. The magic within me surged, and I opened my eyes to see my light blazing out from my hands and penetrating the mist.

With a loud snarl, Derrit charged toward me, his eyes blazing with fury. I stood my ground, my body enveloped in a bright light. As he neared me, I raised one of my hands, and another beam of light shot out, hitting Derrit square in the chest. The mist flickered out for a moment as he stumbled backward, crumbling in pain.

While I could've used more of my power, my wolf urged me to shift. Fur sprouted from my body, my nails extending into sharp claws, and a ferocious roar erupted from my throat, one that my body had never once made before.

The power of the moon flowed through me, making me faster, stronger, and even more agile than I had been in my entire life. I had trained nonstop in my old pack, all by myself, in order to feel accepted.

Who knew that I had been stronger than them all along?

"Go!" I screamed through the mind link to the pack. *"Take cover."*

"We live together. We fight together. We die together," Stone said through the mind link.

And then, like a symphony, the pack repeated it back to him. Back to me.

My heart raced in exhilaration, as I'd never felt so much ... togetherness, and I bared my teeth at Derrit, readying to attack with Stone and an entire pack behind me who had vowed to fight by my side.

I honestly didn't know the power Derrit was about to unlock or how strong he truly was. But I refused to back down from him now. I had a pack, a mate, and possibly a family to protect. Derrit would not take that away from me. I had hoped for this for decades before meeting Stone.

He unleashed a wave of dark energy toward me, the sound nearly busting my eardrums, but I swiftly dodged it. The magic grazed against my fur, searing it right off. I regained my balance and countered with a burst of my own lunar energy, the magic bright white.

Instead of dodging mine, he used his magic as a shield. When the forces collided, a shock wave rocked the entire forest. The trees around us shook violently, their leaves rustling, their branches cracking, and some even falling.

Derrit easily advanced toward me, using his magic to push me back. His dark magic grew stronger with every step he took, and I … I feared that I didn't have any more to give. If he reached me, this would all be over.

I had to act before it was too late. Before we lost for good.

After a deep breath, I closed my eyes and focused my energy on the moon coursing through my veins. I had never had the strength, the courage, or the mere need to survive as I had right now. A bubble formed around me, like a protective shield that Derrit couldn't penetrate, even his strongest dark magic.

Yet he snarled and continued to advance toward me, his face contorted into one of anger and his lips curled into the ugliest of snarls. The closer he approached, the harder it was for me to hold up the pieces of the shield, the strain beginning to take its toll on me. My magic weakened.

How much longer can I keep this up?

Once I scanned the forest, I caught a glimpse of Stone behind Derrit, killing Derrit's second strongest wolf, which must've been his beta. Stone spit his throat out of his mouth, blood covering his fur, then turned toward Derrit.

Hopefully, I had enough left in me until Stone could save me.

Suddenly, a ring of fire blazed around the forest, engulfing the trees and locking all of us inside it. Beads of sweat dripped off my fur, the heat from the flames almost making standing in it unbearable. But it only seemed to make Stone stronger.

It had been days, maybe weeks, since he had told me, but Stone had mentioned that he had contracted with a demon so he could walk through fire, so he could *survive* through fire, and maybe even so his power was strengthened through fire.

This fight was far from over. It was just getting started now.

My mate was at his strongest, and he was ready to kill.

CHAPTER
FORTY-FIVE

STONE

A RING of orange fire burned around the battlefield. The flames ate up the trees and turned them to ashes within minutes. Walls of almost unbearable heat hit me one after another after another as the green grass blackened.

My pain consumed me, growing hotter and stronger by the moment. Flames crackled around me. I inhaled the smoke and glared at my brother through stinging eyes.

Dead.

By the end of today, Derrit would be a dead man. I'd make sure of it.

Surrounded by dark, swirling mist that almost shielded his entire body, Derrit stood as smug as ever. He would never let his face be covered, as that was what he used to taunt me with. That smirk, those devilish eyes.

After growling, I transformed into my wolf form and leaped toward my brother. If he wanted a war, then I would give him a war. I didn't care what kind of magic-wielding wolf he could transform into. I had made a pact with a demon of fire, and I planned to use my abilities as much as I needed in order to defeat him and protect my pack.

My canines sliced into one of the dark mist appendages he wielded, and I ripped it right off him. As if it were alive, the darkness screeched under my teeth and disintegrated into thousands of brittle ashes, drifting away in the fire's wind.

I lunged at him again, chomping away at his dark magic as Zuri fought him head-on, the brightness from her wolf shining through the darkness *and* brighter than the fire around us. She moved like a ball of light.

The force of my second attack pushed Derrit back several feet across the forest floor and toward the edge of the fire's ring. I sprinted at him again as the fire licked my paws, and suddenly, my fur ignited in flames. While it would've seared off the fur and melted the skin of any other wolf, the demon inside me only made me stronger.

After seizing his dark mist between my teeth again, I slammed it into the ground. A shock wave traveled up the darkness and to his body, banging his entire body into the ground once more, his bones cracking from the impact.

Flames popped. Forests burned. And ashes created a heavy fog that sat across the battlefield. The closer I approached Derrit, the quieter my surroundings were, until the wolves' howls became muffled, and the hum of fire seemed to be the only thing bringing me back down to Durnbone.

Derrit groaned and pulled all the black mist back into his body, his dulling eyes refilling with energy once more. Another low growl escaped my throat, and I lurched at him again, this time sinking my canines into his thigh and ripping out a chunk of his flesh.

When I attempted to bite him a second time, he dodged my attack and jumped to his feet. The wound healed almost instantly, the darkness filling the once-empty space where his muscle had been.

"Very well done, little brother," he hummed. "Much stronger than last time."

In my wolf form, I snarled at him and lowered into an offensive position. The thunderous collapse of a tree suddenly snapped me back into reality, where noises weren't muffled anymore, and I could hear the screams of my packmates all around us.

Derrit's body suddenly disappeared and then reappeared behind Zuri in a half-man, half-wolf form. Darkness swirled around him, and he seized my mate, one hand on her neck, the other on her belly, his claws digging into her flesh.

"This is what you deserve, Stone," Derrit roared. "You've always been so prideful to be on your own, so fucking excited to have a family that wasn't like me or Dad. And now … you'll never have that. I'll make sure of it, *brother*."

Before I could stop him, he ripped his claws right into Zuri's belly. Blood spewed out of her stomach, her intestines falling out and onto the ground. He pulled his hand back and dropped her womb with the smallest of pups inside it.

My mind emptied as I stared at her pup—*our pup*—lying in a puddle of Zuri's blood on the ground, its small body barely the size of a coin and curled up in a ball. Heart dropping, I stared at the baby and fell to my knees.

No.

No. This can't be happening.

"Your line ends here." Derrit laughed. "Now, she'll never be able to bear you pups. And if she can't bear your pups, then she's worthless to you. To your pack. And to any other man in existence. Zuri is as good as a dead woman."

FORTY-SIX

ZURI

STONE SHIFTED and fell to the ground, screaming my name and grasping some woman's intestines scattered across the dirt. A blood-soaked acorn lay in his palm as heartbreaking howls escaped his throat repeatedly.

I stared in horror across the forest, his pain rushing through my chest. Derrit must've … used his magic to make Stone see something. Something so bad that it forced Stone to break into a hundred little pieces.

"Zuri!" Stone screamed, crawling closer toward the woman who Derrit had just killed. The ring of fire around Stone slowly burned out until he lay in the middle of a brittle, blackened battlefield as his warriors died for us. "Zuri! Come back to me!"

As if he were some sort of god, Derrit smirked down at my mate.

How dare he! Pain, agony, and fury flooded through my system, some of Stone's but mostly my own. *I will kill Derrit for whatever he has done to him!*

The man who I had once feared lay in a puddle of blood, clutching a corpse because he thought it was me. And what did the acorn symbolize? I didn't have time to figure it out. I refused to let Derrit lay a finger on him.

He might've been able to seep into Stone's mind. But he couldn't get to me.

I transformed and ran toward Stone, ignoring the sharp thorns and branches that impaled into my skin. My heart beat in my damn ears, my dry throat closing. I needed to get him to safety before he really died in the hands of this devil.

"Stone!" I shouted, but he continued to hold the woman and sob my name.

"I couldn't save her," he cried when I reached him. "I couldn't save my mate or our pup!"

Tears burned my eyes, and I pulled him behind me. His pain and sorrow cut through me like a jagged dagger. But underneath all of it, my anger blazed like a fucking wildfire, reigniting the flames that had once burned the forest to ashes.

The acorn … Derrit must've made Stone think he had killed our baby. My heart raced at the thought, and I placed my free hand on my belly, feeling the slightest of heartbeats within it. Derrit knew that we were trying to get pregnant, and he had used it against Stone.

He had broken him down over the past few weeks, but I was stronger than ever.

When I released my hold on Stone, he collapsed back down, clutching the woman and the acorn, unable to even hear me, unable to process anything other than his grief. My teeth lengthened into canines as Derrit's eyes shone with malice.

"You're going to pay for what you've done," I growled, my voice low.

Derrit's smirk faded slightly. "And I suppose *you'll* be the one to do that? I don't—"

Before he could finish his sentence, my body seemed to move on its own. I leaped up, my toes floating off the ground and I ascended into the sky. Power built inside me with every foot I rose in the air until the force was so strong that my bones could barely contain it.

With every passing moment, the once-bright battlefield darkened, as if my body had created an eclipse over Durnbone.

When my gaze landed on Stone, who sat helpless at Derrit's feet, I detonated like a bomb, moonlight exploding out from my skin. The light itself ate up any of the dark magic that Derrit wielded, completely disintegrating his mist and any tattoos that had been inked onto his skin.

Pain from a thousand wolves in battle scattered through me, stabbing me like a sharp knife repeatedly. Another wave of energy passed through me, hitting Derrit right in the chest and sending him miles across the forest, away from the battle.

I moved through the air with ease. I immediately locked on to him, focusing all of my energy on the center of Derrit's chest as he stood up on shaky legs and held his hands up, as if attempting to shoot his magic back out at me.

But his magic had disappeared.

For the first time, he was helpless. And if I had learned anything from him, then I should prey on helpless men like him. Because helpless men like *him* deserved every last bit of pain that they gave to others.

Another beam of power zapped out of my body. I hit one of his arms and blew it off.

He howled in pain.

I lifted my finger and shot off his remaining three limbs in one go, and then I landed on the ground before him, still raging with fury. Derrit deserved this more than anyone I had ever met.

"S-stop!" Derrit shouted, just a head and torso. "Please, stop! I surren—"

Before he could say another word, I placed my hand on the center of his chest. "Shh, shh, shh. You've done very well, Derrit. Much better than you did last time. Don't worry. It'll all be over very soon."

"Please, Zuri! I'll do anything to—"

A shock wave of pressure burst through my palm, and Derrit's chest exploded.

"You evil, pathetic bastard," I growled at his corpse. "Stone and I are unstoppable together. It was weak of you to think that either one of us would ever let you get in the middle of what we have. Not even life or death will stop us."

CHAPTER
FORTY-SEVEN

ZURI

ONCE WE DEFEATED the remaining wolves, who had either submitted to us or died, I hurried over to Stone, who still sat in tears on the ground beside hundreds of werewolf corpses. My chest tightened at the sight of how broken he looked right now.

I had always thought he was undefeatable, but I knew now that if I was gone, then he'd be too. At least his mind wouldn't survive in this world any longer. He'd be completely and utterly broken and blank.

"Stone," I whispered, gently separating him from the woman's body. "Stone, it's me."

"Zuri!" he cried, attempting to reach for the woman again.

Pain shot through my body—both his pain and mine because he didn't recognize me. We had spent so much time together, and Derrit's magic had ruined it all! He was dead, yet his power continued to exist in the real world.

Had he cursed Stone to a life of … heartbreak?

And in turn, cursed me as well?

"I'll bring him home," James said. "Get him out of here, and maybe he'll think clearly."

While I wished that he'd recognize me, Derrit's dark magic still had a hold on him, and he needed to rest. I had a pack to take care of, especially now that my mate couldn't think straight. I would get them back to our property and have their wounds healed.

James picked up Stone in a fireman's carry and headed back toward the property.

"Is there anything we can do?" Maxine said from behind me.

I twirled around to see the entire gang—Sina and her four wolves, Maxine and Xorgor, Olenna and a reluctant Carve beside her—all beaten and bruised.

My eyes widened slightly, and I sucked in a breath. "You all came?"

"Been here from the beginning, killing those bastards," Carve said, twirling a knife.

"Actually," Olenna interjected, "Carve didn't get here until after the battle began."

"I was here the whole fucking time, Olenna. Just because you can't see—"

"Go flirt somewhere else," Sina said, gently pushing them toward the bodies on the ground. "Or make yourselves useful by piling up the bodies and burning them. Don't want this place to become infested with rodents."

Once the bickering died out between the two, I smiled softly and turned back to the others. "Thank you all for coming to help out. I lost it when Derrit captured Stone's mind. And I ..." Tears welled up in my eyes. "I hope he returns to normal."

Maxine cleared her throat. "Why don't you head back to be with him and your pack?"

"We'll clean up here," Sina said.

"Are you sure?" I asked.

I had destroyed everything, and they were asking me to leave the mess to someone else.

Sina nudged me in the direction of home. "Positive."

After she convinced me, I walked around the pile of dead

bodies that Olenna and Carve had begun piling and jogged to catch up with a few of my packmates that had been wounded during the fight. We walked in a comfortable silence to the property, and then they bowed their heads and entered the pack hospital.

I had done a great job at holding back the tears—and the fear that I had lost my mate forever to the darkness—until I stepped into the pack house. As soon as the door shut, tears sprang from my eyes, and I dropped to my knees and sobbed.

And I sobbed and sobbed and sobbed until nothing was left.

When I couldn't cry anymore, I lifted myself off the ground and stood on wobbly legs. I headed up the stairs to our bedroom and hoped that James had brought Stone right back home and not to the hospital. I wanted to spend some time with him first, see if I could heal him myself.

"We've been examining him since he returned," Ifa said inside the room.

"It doesn't look like just any dark magic that Derrit used, but dark magic from the Dark One."

"The Dark One?" I repeated, shaking my head. "What does that mean?"

The sisters shared a look.

"The Dark One is a god who used to thrive a long, long time ago," Ifa said. "When our previous sister was alive, they used to … have relations together. He was sorta her mate in some ways."

"But we haven't seen him since she died," Shivani continued.

"We theorized that the Dark One had died too. That their souls passed together since they were so tied to each other." Ifa stared down at my mate and shook her head. "But now, we know that isn't true. He's back."

"So, what does this mean?" I whispered. "Is he an enemy?"

"It's hard to tell, but his magic lives on while Derrit is gone." Shivani frowned. "Usually, whenever a mortal contracts with a god or goddess, once the mortal dies, all the magic that he or she performed vanishes."

I pushed some tears off my cheek and walked toward him. "Then, why isn't it gone?"

Again, the sisters shared another pitiful look.

"We don't know."

"He'll come back around," Shivani said.

Ifa nodded. "At some point."

After sitting beside his sobbing body, after feeling all his pain, I grabbed his hand and prayed that he'd return to me. He couldn't be like this forever, could he? If he stayed like this, he wouldn't get to see me go through this pregnancy or have our pup. He wouldn't get to be a father the way that I knew he wanted.

When he didn't awaken from just my touch, I placed his hand on my belly to see if he could feel the second faint heartbeat inside my stomach. To see if he could feel our pup growing inside me. It was a last-ditch effort.

"Please awaken, Stone," I whispered. "I can't lose you."

CHAPTER
FORTY-EIGHT

STONE

THE FAINTEST OF heartbeats fluttered against my palm.

I sprawled my hand across someone's stomach, blinked a few times, and then shifted my gaze upward to Zuri, who stood over me. My eyes widened slightly, and I sat straight up in the bed, heart pounding. Stars danced in my vision, and suddenly, pain split through my head.

"Thank Goddess," Zuri murmured, sitting beside me and gently motioning for me to lie back down. "You're going to hurt yourself, Stone. You've been out of it for almost an hour now."

"Y-y-you're alive," I murmured, resting my head against the pillow and staring at her.

How was she alive? I had seen Derrit kill her, rip out her womb, and murder our baby.

My gaze dropped to her belly, which didn't even look like it had been wounded at all. I squeezed my eyes closed and shook my head. None of this made any sense. She was dead. And I didn't … we didn't …

"Derrit is dead," Zuri whispered. "You don't have to worry about him anymore."

"Did you—" I began, but then visions began playing through my head, as if I hadn't seen them before right now. Visions of Zuri floating in the sky, her chest burning as bright as the moon, tearing Derrit to pieces. "You … killed him."

"I did."

While I was so fucking proud of Zuri, I had been completely useless. My contract with the devil had been useless. My strength had been useless. My blood—that of an alpha—had been useless. I hadn't been enough to protect my mate and my pack.

She pulled me into a tight hug, one of her tears falling onto my cheek. "I'm so happy you're safe and back to normal. I thought I had lost you for good. I don't know … I don't know what I'd do without you."

"Maybe you should go get him some water and a doctor," a woman said to our left.

Zuri glanced over at the tall, slender woman and nodded. "You're right. I'll be back."

Before I could get out another word, Zuri scurried out of the room and down the hallway. I winced from the pain shooting through my head as another vision of Zuri clutching her belly during the fight drifted through my mind.

Did Zuri … was she pregnant? Really pregnant?

"Do you think she knows yet?" one of the women whispered to the other.

I pushed myself to a seated position and leaned against the headboard. "Knows what?"

Both the women stared over at me through wide eyes.

"You can … hear us?" one said.

"Yes …" I murmured, blinking my eyes through the pain. "Can see you too."

The women, who seemed like sisters, shared a look with each other and then walked to my bedside and stared down at me quizzically. With their brow furrowed, they stalked around me and hummed.

"Why do you think he can see us now?" one asked.

"The dark magic perhaps?"

"We're only visible to those that are worthy, and he hasn't been worthy before."

"Ifa," the other said, "you literally paired Zuri with him as mates."

The other rolled her eyes. "For mating and babies! Not for seeing us in our true form."

I cleared my throat. "I'm still here."

The older, skinnier sister sat at my bedside. "I'm Shivani, and that's Ifa. We're Zuri's sisters."

"And your goddesses," Ifa said.

Shivani rolled her eyes again. "Don't mind her. She loves being dramatic."

"I do not!" Ifa said, throwing up her arms. "I just want to know why he can see us."

"He can see us because, now, he is worthy, sister," Shivani said. "Stop it."

After moving closer to me, Ifa looked into my eyes and placed her fingers inches from my face. The pain began evaporating from my head, as if being drawn out, and then a black mist began rising from my skin and swirling in the air. Shivani's eyes widened.

"What is it?" I asked.

"The Dark One. He's here."

"The Dark One?" I repeated after they didn't continue explaining.

Where had I heard that name before? It sounded so familiar.

Shivani grabbed Ifa's hand. "We must tell Zuri."

Before either of them could run off to find my mate and tell her anything, I snapped my hand around Ifa's wrist and yanked her back. The black mist wrapped around her forearm like a rope, one I wasn't controlling.

"What is it?" I asked.

The door reopened, and Zuri stopped in her tracks with water in her hand and a doctor behind her. The doctor's eyes widened, and she shuffled backward.

"What happened to him? He looks like—"

"The Dark One," Shivani said to Zuri, "is here."

"He never dies," Ifa said, her flesh burning underneath the mist.

I released her wrist, and the mist swarmed back into my body.

"Just as gods and goddesses never die, the Dark One doesn't either," Ifa continued. "His spirit moves from one body to the next once the time has come. At least, that was the ancient myth that I learned. But when our other sister died, I don't know... I didn't think it was possible. I didn't have hope in it anymore."

"W-what else does the myth say?" Zuri asked.

My throat dried, and suddenly, Grandma Bee's prophecy finally made sense. She had talked about a goddess and a dark spirit saving our pack from all the evil, the prophecy that she had seen in her dreams since she had been a girl.

"If the Dark One doesn't see that a body is fit for him, he leaves it behind," I finished.

"Derrit wasn't contracted with the Dark One," Shivani whispered, as if it all made sense.

"Derrit *was* the Dark One," Ifa whispered.

I stared down at my tattoos that began lifting off my body and forming a dark mist around me. It swirled through the air and then swarmed around Zuri, pieces of it clinging to her and drawing her closer to me. If what they had said was true and if the Dark One had really chosen not to be with Derrit anymore, then that meant ...

It had chosen me.

CHAPTER
FORTY-NINE

STONE

"WHAT DOES THIS MEAN?" Zuri asked with her brow furrowed. She moved closer to me and gently caressed the stubble on my face, her gaze flickering up to Shivani and Ifa. "I … does this mean that he …"

"Can live for as long as you do?" Shivani asked. "Possibly."

Ifa snickered. "As long as he doesn't anger the Dark One."

With her lips quivering, Zuri threw her arms around my shoulders and tackled me back onto the bed, sobbing into the crook of my neck. "Oh my Goddess. I can't believe this. I don't think I would have been able to go on without you. Ever."

"We'll give you two some privacy," Shivani said, tugging her unwilling sister out of the room.

Ifa dug her heels into the ground, wiggling her eyebrows at us and mouthing the words, *Make more babies.*

Once they disappeared and shut the door behind them, I curled my arms around Zuri's body and pulled her closer to me. "I already told you that I wouldn't ever leave you, *mate.* You're all mine. No matter what happens to my body or my soul, I'll be with you."

"You don't understand," she whispered, straddling my lap. "I need you. I can't do this ..."

Before she could finish her sentence, she pressed her lips together and stared at me through teary eyes.

I tucked some strands of hair behind her ear and smiled softly at her. "You can't do what without me? You stand strong by yourself."

"I can't raise a pup without you," she said.

"A pup?" A low chuckle escaped my mouth. "Are you pregnant?"

And while it seemed so far-fetched because we had only really started trying a couple of days ago, I faintly remembered my hand against Zuri's belly right before I snapped out of the trance. I'd thought that Derrit was making it all up.

But ...

I sat up taller and grasped her hips in my hand. "Are you really pregnant?"

A small smile crossed her lips. "Maybe."

All the anguish that Derrit had put me through for those few hours, all the heartbreak ... it all seemed to vanish instantly as that single word left Zuri's mouth. I placed my hand on her belly and felt the faintest of heartbeats.

"We're having a pup," I whispered to myself.

After I had left Derrit and my father, I'd never thought that I'd find someone who loved me enough to give me a pup. I thought I would have to force my mate to even want to be with me. And while Zuri had come with a fight, it was a fight that I'd take any day.

Because we were having a pup. A pup!

Warmth exploded through my chest, and I pulled her into a tight hug. "Mine."

She wrapped her arms around my shoulders and settled herself on my lap comfortably. "After Shivani and Ifa told me that I'd live for thousands of years, I feared that I wouldn't be able to do anything without you. But … we get to raise a pup together. A freaking pup!"

"I promise to be there with you through everything," I murmured against her mark.

I held her, and I held her, and I held her until she finally pulled away.

"We might have a pup, but we have problems we must resolve before that. Like … what're we going to do about Durnbone?" she asked.

"We'll help rebuild the parts that Derrit destroyed." I pulled her closer to me and rested my forehead on hers, unable to contain my excitement. "Because, together, we are now unstoppable, Zuri."

"Unstoppable," she repeated. "I like the sound of that."

"You'd better because you're not getting rid of me. You have to deal with my crazy ass for the rest of eternity. We're bound together by the heavens, by the goddesses. You are mine, and I am forever yours."

She smiled. "Does that mean … I'm going to have to bathe in the ashes of our enemies?"

"Oh, for sure, *mate*." I chuckled. "We'll bathe in them together."

To continue reading My Bad Boy Alpha: The Epilogue, subscribe to my newsletter!

ALSO BY EMILIA ROSE

Paranormal Romance

Submitting to the Alpha

Come Here, Kitten

My Werewolf Professor

The Twins

Four Masked Wolves

Monster Lover

Contemporary Romance

Stepbrother

Poison

The Bad Boy

Detention

Excite Me

Mafia Boss

Mafia Toy

ABOUT THE AUTHOR

Emilia Rose is a USA Today bestselling author of steamy romance. She loves writing about dirty-talking bad boys who are obsessed with innocent, and sometimes insecure, virgin heroines. She currently lives in a small town in Connecticut USA with her husband and three playful cats.

Join Emilia's newsletter for exclusive giveaways, early chapter releases, and more!

www.ingramcontent.com/pod-product-compliance
Lightning Source LLC
Chambersburg PA
CBHW020026310726
48970CB00007B/2209